WAVING,
NOT
DROWNING

By the same author:

Last Seen Wearing Trainers

WAVING, NOT DROWNING

Rosie Rushton

Andersen Press • London

First published in 2003 by
Andersen Press Limited,
20 Vauxhall Bridge Road, London SW1V 2SA
www.andersenpress.co.uk

British Library Cataloguing in Publication Data available
ISBN 1 84270 237 8

Typeset by FiSH Books, London WC1
Printed and bound in Great Britain by Mackays of Chatham Ltd.,
Chatham, Kent

To Anne Goodman, without whom this book could never have been written, and to the pupils of Campion School, Bugbroke, for their insight and perception into the realities of being 16 today

1

It happened every time. He would reach the corner of Elterwater Walk and Kendal Street and then he would stop running. It was stupid really, considering the whole point of the exercise was to get home as quickly as possible and sort out whatever mess was waiting for him this time. It was just that he knew that once he turned the corner and looked down the long row of dreary terraced houses to Number 18, he wouldn't be able to pretend any longer. Daydreams didn't survive for long in Elterwater Walk.

In order to put off the inevitable, Jay always did one of two things. If it was raining, he slumped down on the broken bench inside the bus shelter and tried not to inhale the stench of stale beer and urine. Then he would close his eyes and picture his nan standing at the front door, smartly dressed and totally together – just like she used to be. Creative Visualisation, it was called – he'd read about it in a magazine in the dentist's waiting room. Apparently, if you imagined things often enough and hard enough they came true.

It hadn't worked so far.

He didn't always stop at the bus shelter. If it was dry, he crossed over the street and stood outside P and J Stores, reading the cards stuck with curling sellotape to the inside of the window. *'Babysitter wanted – £2 an hour.' 'Mr Fixit, odd jobs done – no task too small.' 'Fed up with being fat? Lose weight fast with Fataway Fitness Plan. Phone Marilyn on 01404 556557.'*

He would stand there and imagine writing his own card. 'Boy, aged 16, seeks someone – anyone – to get him out of here. Live-in post; hours never-ending, pay nothing at all.'

Today he added another sentence to his imaginary advertisement. 'Suitable post for someone who doesn't want a life.'

The sheer absurdity of it brought a faint smile to his lips. Mr Dawson, his maths teacher, said that every problem had a solution; it was just a case of applying your mind to it. Well, he was wrong. Solutions always depended on everything else being in place; you had to have money, or friends, or no conscience at all and then you could work most things out. Jay didn't have cash, or any really close mates – not the kind you would bare your soul to, at any rate. All he had was Nan. She was all he'd ever had – well, no – that wasn't strictly true. He had had Mum way back, but he could only remember her in the briefest of flashes. If it hadn't been for all the photographs of her round the house, he guessed he'd have forgotten her altogether. After all, he had only been three years old when she and his father were killed.

There was no photo of his father.

'Least said about him the better,' Nan used to say. 'It's not as if they were married or anything. Thank God.'

Until he was about twelve, he'd pestered her to know more. Now he didn't bother. It never got him anywhere and besides, he had more important things to worry about.

So it was just him and Nan.

'We'll be all right, little man,' she used to croon to him when he was tiny. 'We'll do just fine.' And they had.

Until last Easter. It was when he thought about last Easter that his conscience started rearing its head. He should never have gone on the field trip because, deep down, he had known things weren't quite right. He couldn't put his finger on it; Nan had always been a bit dotty, a bit forgetful and she'd always been the sort of person who, once she'd got an idea in her head, wouldn't rest until she had carried it out. Gritty, her friends called her. The people on the receiving end of her outbursts had ruder words to describe her behaviour.

Jay couldn't help thinking that, if he'd been at home in April, he could have stopped her doing what she did, or even taken the blame himself. But by the time he got back, it was too late.

The memory was enough to jolt him out of his daydreams and send him belting down Elterwater Walk to his house. He guessed the town planners, or whichever sad souls had named the streets in Harpleton, had thought that giving the road the name of some beauty spot up North would somehow make the place better. The whole Belgate estate was like that: Kendal Close, Windermere Way, Ullswater Court. Trouble was, they'd reckoned without the litter blowing haphazardly across the pavement, the empty drink cans rusting slowly in the gutters, the crude graffiti scrawled on the whitewashed wall of the chip shop. Even the tiny patches of weed-ridden turf that made up the front gardens of the houses were, more often than not, obscured by the clutter of bicycles and motorbikes, or bags of rubbish spilling out of dustbins.

At least his house wasn't like that. Nan had always been house proud; everything had to be immaculate. Instead of grass, Number 18 sported a neat patch of gravel with a lavender bush in the middle. There had been some terracotta flower pots with purple and yellow pansies, but stuff that was breakable never lasted long in the Belgate estate. Nan had talked of getting a bay tree, whatever that might be, but it had never materialised. Jay guessed bay trees must be expensive. At least they were on the best side of the street, the one overlooking the bottom end of Abbey Park.

'Nan! It's me! I'm back!'

In the split second that passed between shouting out and hearing the front door slam behind him, Jay's heart missed a beat.

'Your grandmother phoned...'

The school secretary's words were echoing in his head – but not quite as loudly as the memory of the titter that rippled around 10D.

'Ah diddums...what does Granny want this time, then?...have you got your vest on, Jay?'

Even thinking about it brought the heat flooding to his cheeks.

'Nan?'

From the tiny kitchen at the end of the hallway came the sound of faint humming.

Promising, he told himself encouragingly, as he pushed open the door. If everything was OK, he could grab a can of cola and be back at school in time for afternoon registration; if not . . .

His grandmother was sitting at the breakfast bar, chopping carrots.

'Jay!' she beamed, dropping the knife and heaving herself off the stool. 'What are you doing home at this time?'

Jay felt his shoulders relax. She looked OK; neatly dressed, mug of tea on the table, the *Daily Mail* folded open at the horoscope. She was fine. What had he been worrying about?

'You phoned,' he said gently. 'Remember?'

'Phoned?' Her forehead wrinkled in a frown. 'I didn't phone.'

'Yes,' he urged. 'You phoned the school—'

'Don't be so ridiculous!' she retorted. 'Why on earth would I do that?'

'Well, I don't know, do I?' He didn't mean to snap but he couldn't help himself. He was missing lunch and Science Club – neither of which mattered that much; but he was also missing out on the chance to see Fiona – and that did.

He liked to pretend that Fiona Bayliss was his girlfriend. Of course, she wasn't, and never would be; the only reason she took any notice of him was because Mr Cole had decided to team him up with her and Reena Banerjee for the Science Competition. Besides, she was tall and had gorgeous dark hair, and he was small and gingery and covered with freckles. Girls never looked at him twice; but he could dream. Maybe, if he got a move on and dealt with Nan, he could still catch her before lessons started.

And then he'd ask her to go to the Town Fair with him. If he dared.

Which, of course, he wouldn't.

'So what was it all about then, Nan?' he repeated. 'Why did you phone?'

'I didn't phone!' Nan's voice was taking on that pleading note, like a small kid trying to wheedle its way out of trouble. 'I didn't!'

'Yes, you . . .' He stopped. What was the point? If he went on about it, she'd only get upset and then he'd be here forever.

'Maybe the secretary got the wrong person,' he ended lamely. 'Not to worry.'

He gave her a quick kiss on the cheek.

'Got to go,' he muttered. 'I'll be back about five.'

'Well, don't go without your games kit this time!' his gran interrupted. 'It's on your bed.'

Jay stared at her and a great wave of relief washed over him. OK, so he didn't need games kit today, and it was only on his bed because he'd forgotten to put it in the washing bin, but at least it explained things.

'So that's what you phoned about!' he cried, giving her a hug. 'See, you did phone!'

The moment the words were out he regretted them.

'You think I'd waste good money phoning a forgetful kid like you!' she snapped. 'Your memory's your problem, not mine!'

Jay forced himself to grin. He was used to deflecting his grandmother's sudden outbursts.

'Yeah, you're right!' he nodded, tapping the side of his head and raising his eyebrows. 'I'll just go and get it and be off, then!'

'That's a good boy!' his nan beamed, her mood switching back as swiftly as it had changed. 'Want something to eat?'

Jay shook his head.

'No time,' he told her. 'I'll get my kit and split, thanks!'

He ran upstairs two at a time, grabbed the kit, stuffed it under his bed where she wouldn't find it, darted into the loo, and then sped downstairs again.

'I've done you a sandwich anyway,' Nan said, thrusting a foil wrapped package into his hands. 'Growing boys need to eat.'

Growing? I wish, Jay thought.

'You can take it with you. Mind how you go!'

'Thanks, Nan! See you!' Jay felt almost lightheaded with relief. He'd got himself into a state over nothing. Nan was fine; just a bit forgetful. All that other business had just been a blip.

He glanced at his watch. With a bit of luck, he'd make it back to school in time. That was one advantage of living only a few streets away.

He was out of breath by the time he reached the gates of Bishop Andrew Upper School, but there were still clusters of kids ambling through the swing doors into the Arts block, so he guessed the second bell hadn't gone.

'What you got there, then?'

He didn't have to turn round to know who was asking the question. Rick Barnes. And if Rick was there, it was an odds-on certainty Matt Cooper was there too.

He quickened his pace without glancing behind him.

'I said, what you got there then?'

With one stride, Rick was in front of him, blocking his path and gesturing towards the somewhat squashed package in Jay's hand.

'Just a sandwich,' Jay said as casually as he could.

'We were just saying how hungry we were, isn't that right, Matt?'

Rick nudged his mate.

'You can have it if you want,' Jay replied. With Rick standing this close, he suddenly wasn't hungry anyway.

'Really?' Rick's upper lip curled as he towered over Jay. 'I'd have thought a little midget like you needed all the food he could get.'

Jay swallowed. At five foot four he was the smallest boy in his year and scrawny with it. He didn't like to be reminded of the fact.

'Suit yourself!' He shrugged, feigning a bravado he certainly didn't feel.

To his intense relief, the registration bell shrilled. He made a feeble attempt to push past the two boys.

'Not so fast!' Rick ordered. 'Give it here!'

Jay handed the package over, and slowly, his eyes never leaving Jay's face, Rick peeled back the silver foil.

'What the . . . ?'

The package fell to the ground as Rick recoiled in disgust.

'Yuck!' Matt took a step backwards.

'That is so gross!' Rick clamped his hand to his mouth.

Jay looked down.

The bread was green with mould, its crusts curling with age.

His stomach lurched. He should have known. It had all been going so well. Too well.

'I guess you thought you were being clever, didn't you?' snarled Rick, recovering himself. 'Offering me that revolting muck? You little toe rag!'

He clamped a hand on Jay's shoulder and Matt took a step closer.

'I didn't know!' gasped Jay, glancing frantically round the playground. 'Honestly – my na—'

He stopped.

What was there to say? The truth was out of the question.

'I don't like guys who try to put one over on me, do I, Matt?' Rick snarled.

'You don't, Rick, nah!' Matt replied.

'Still,' Rick went on, pulling a piece of gum from his pocket and unwrapping it slowly. 'I guess it's only to be expected. Garbage eating garbage!'

He glanced at Matt and dead on cue, he burst into peals of appreciative laughter.

'You'd better clear this up, Squirt!' Rick jeered, shoving Jay in the chest and kicking the sandwich with the toe of his grubby trainer.

It flew in an arc for several feet and its filling splattered over the damp tarmac of the playground.

In that moment, Jay wanted to die.

Chocolate buttons, raw carrot and a slice of uncooked bacon stared up mockingly at him.

'What the . . . ?'

Jay didn't wait to hear more of Rick's response. As he belted towards the swing doors and into the comparative safety of Reception, it wasn't just shame and misery he felt. It was undiluted, red hot anger.

She'd done it again. She'd humiliated him in front of the two people most able to make his life a misery. How could she do that to him? Forgetful was one thing, but no one could be that dumb, no one.

In that moment, he hated his nan as he'd never hated anyone before.

★ ★ ★

'Here lies Frederick Thomas Buckley, dearly loved son of Sidney and Blanche Buckley, born October 3rd 1834, died August 2nd 1850 in tragic . . .'

Lyall Porter squatted down and picked at the ingrained moss on the crumbling headstone.

'. . . *circ . . .*'

He fumbled in the pocket of his jeans and pulled out his penknife. Flipping open the blade, he gouged at the moss, feeling the shape of the carved letters as he went.

'. . . *circumstances! Died August 2nd 1850 in tragic circumstances,*' he read out loud and then looked round hastily, in case anyone had heard him.

But for once, the windswept churchyard was deserted. It was too cold for office workers to eat their sandwiches outdoors and his words were merely lost in the drone of traffic crawling past the church towards the multi-storey car park.

He scraped away at some more of the moss.

'*Deeply mourned by his loving parents and . . .*'

A final dig with the blade and a lump of moss fell at his feet.

'. . . *sister Joan. Rest in peace.*'

He stared at the words and all the old familiar feelings rose up inside him. He could feel his heart rate quickening, the tell-tale pricking behind his eyes, the taste of blood as he involuntarily bit down hard on his bottom lip.

'*Tragic circumstances . . .*'

The words echoed in his heart and his heart beat louder to keep in time with them.

'*Trag-ic cir-cum-stances, tra-gic cir-cum-stances . . .*'

For a moment, he wasn't standing in the shadow of St Giles's church, its pathway splattered with pigeon droppings and the odd puddle of congealing vomit left by last night's revellers. He was standing on a strange doorstep, shivering with fear, his hand going numb because the woman with the red hair was holding onto it so tightly.

'... *poor little chap... tragic really... still, he'll be all right with you...*'

But he hadn't been all right. He hadn't been right ever since.

'... *deeply mourned by his loving parents and sister Joan,*' he read again, peering at the worn and faded lettering.

'Well, lucky bloody him!'

He yelled out the words and a clutch of pigeons pecking round a nearby rubbish bin fluttered up into the air in alarm.

He stood up, clenched his fists and began drumming them against his thighs. October 1834 to August 1850! Maths wasn't his best subject but it didn't take him long to work out that this Frederick guy – the one under the mound of earth – was the same age as him. Just a few weeks short of sixteen.

Dead at sixteen. Everything over and done with.

What, Lyall wondered, squatting down once more beside the overgrown grave, does dead feel like? No one ever comes back to tell you, so how does anyone know? They tell you that once people are dead they are at peace, but how the hell do they know that? They probably just make it up, like they make up all their other platitudes; the 'Lyall, we understand how you're feeling' and 'Lyall, we're here for you; you only have to ask'.

Meaningless, empty words that they say just to make themselves feel good.

He stared at the grave. Would being dead be easier than what he was facing? Was there really a place called heaven where you met everyone you'd ever loved? Because if there was, if he could be really sure, then that's where he'd like to be right now. That would solve everything.

How could they do it to him? Not that he knew exactly what 'it' was yet – he'd only been able to catch a few words of what they'd been muttering about the night before last, when they thought he'd crashed out after the party.

But those words were enough.

'We can't take Lyall . . . you couldn't cope . . . always been a handful . . .' That had been Patrick's gruff voice.

Then Maddy's softer tones, sighing as she spoke. 'I can't cope with all this, not now . . . I guess you're right . . . they'll find something for him . . . after all, he is almost sixteen . . .'

He hadn't heard any more because that was when he'd had to rush to the bathroom to throw up – although whether it had been the Red Bull at Warren's party or the sickening realisation that they were going to chuck him out, he hadn't been able to tell.

He stared at the tombstone, his fists thumping rhythmically on his thighs.

Dead at sixteen. People standing round the grave, crying, feeling guilty, wishing they'd loved you more when they had the chance. That would show them. And if he was dead he wouldn't have to face any of it, wouldn't have to start all over again.

He had really thought that, this time, things might work out OK. It was almost three years now since he'd started living with Maddy and Patrick and it was a whole lot better than the kids' home, or being with that other lot. At least this time he had space to chill out; a bedroom all to himself and even his own TV. And there was no one to wind him up; at all the other places he'd been, there had been other kids and he couldn't stand that. Especially the little ones. The little ones were the worst.

But right now, he'd put up with a houseful of squalling brats rather than face what lay ahead. If Maddy and Patrick didn't want him, no one else would and soon he'd be all on his own.

So what's new? he thought. He'd always been on his own really. Oh, there had been lots of people who had tried to look after him, tried to turn him into a good person. But no proper mum and dad, not like the guy on the gravestone. No sister to cry for him, not any more . . .

Stop. Not allowed. Never think about that.

But the thoughts, once they started, wouldn't stop. They never did; they took on a life of their own and no matter how hard he pushed them away, no matter how much he tried to remember what he was supposed to do, they always won. They were like sharp, black daggers piercing into his head and making him remember.

Well, he wouldn't. He couldn't. He daren't.

He could feel them now, fighting around inside his head, struggling to get out. Each time a dagger pierced his brain, another memory came. Empty rooms with bright lights and horrid smells, whispering voices and pointing fingers, people taking pictures and men shouting.

And then looking for Candy and never finding her.

Candy had loved him, Candy had thought he was an ace person and . . . He could feel the thoughts winning their battle to take him over. He looked frantically round him. He had to find something to do, something that would take all the effort his brain could produce. Because if he didn't, one dagger would jump into his hand and he'd have to smash something to get rid of it and . . .

He rammed his penknife back into his pocket and started off down the path.

Don't walk on the cracks, count the number of blue cars, sing the words of Shiny Vinyl's latest hit backwards; see how far you can hurl that stone . . .

'Hey! You there! What do you think you're doing?'

He was still watching the stone arc upwards past the yew tree when the hand clamped down on his shoulder.

'So it was you, was it?' A short, red-faced man carrying an orange traffic cone had emerged from the gloom of the church porch and was glaring at him from pale piggy eyes.

'What?'

The stone fell with a thud on top of a marble angel by a small grave.

'The windows!' snorted the man, gesturing towards the far end of the church. 'The Apostle's window – smashed last Tuesday! We knew it was vandals and now—'

'That wasn't me!' Lyall protested, jerking his shoulder away from the man's grasp. 'I've never been here before!'

'Nice story, sonny, but it won't wash! I wasn't born yesterday. I've been the verger here for long enough to know a thug when I see one!'

He shouldn't have said that. He really shouldn't. He was making him very angry.

OK. Calm down. Do it like they told you at the therapy centre. Deep breath. Smile.

'And what are you smirking at?'

Not smirking. Smiling.

'OK, so I chucked that stone just now. But it wasn't me that broke the windows.'

Good. Well done, Lyall. Same time next week?

'But you would have done, given half a chance, wouldn't you?' the verger snarled, shoving the traffic cone under one arm and wagging a finger at Lyall. 'I know your type. And why aren't you in school?'

Lyall opened his mouth to reply but the guy was in full flood.

'You kids, you have it all too easy! Nothing to do with your lives so you go around wrecking others. Well, if you were my son—'

That did it. The blackest and sharpest dagger of all was in his hand. He could feel it there, the tip of the blade nipping at his fingers.

He shoved the man away with all the force he could muster.

'I'd rather die than be your son, you old . . .'

The dagger was still there. And it was hurting him.

'You little . . . !' The verger regained his composure and tried to grab Lyall's wrist.

'Get off!' Lyall brought his fist down onto the traffic

cone and then kicked it violently down the path towards the street.

'You don't know me at all!' he yelled. 'You don't know nothing!'

The dagger shrank a little and the pain lessened.

'Is something the matter?'

Lyall wheeled round and found himself just inches from a large bosom on which hung a heavy metal cross. He raised his eyes, took in the clerical collar around which curled a mass of chestnut brown hair and the pale lips which broke into a smile as he lifted his eyes.

'Oh, good morning, Vicar!' The verger's voice changed from coarse gruffness to an oily simper. 'I'm afraid I caught this—'

Lyall didn't wait to hear any more. Cocky little men with an over-inflated sense of their own importance he could deal with; but vicars, of whatever gender, were a different thing altogether.

He belted down the path and out into the street, lashing out at the first thing he saw.

'No Parking. Funeral Expected.'

The metal sign clattered to the ground as Lyall's boot laid into it.

'Come back and chat sometime!'

The words that floated down the path behind him were so absurd that he stopped dead in his tracks, turned and stared back into the graveyard.

'I'm always round about here,' the vicar called. 'Except Fridays. Friday is my day off.'

What was the woman on? He might be heading for a bunch of U grades at GCSE, but he wasn't that stupid. Like he was really going to give her the chance to grass on him. Get real.

She was walking down the path towards him. She was really young and she looked dead laid back. But he wasn't taken in – he knew all about vicars. They said dumb things just like social workers and therapists.

'She's in heaven now, Lyall and you must be happy for her.'

and

'It's not your fault. Don't blame yourself.'

Nice words that meant nothing. It was his fault. And he did blame himself. But he mustn't let the thoughts come.

As he turned to run across the road, two black cars pulled up alongside him blocking his way. As the first one slowed to a halt, he saw the coffin through the smoked glass windows, almost hidden under a mass of flowers and wreaths, its brass handle just visible.

She'd had a coffin.

His throat was closing and his eyes were damp. Sod this! He picked up a Coke can and hurled it at the hearse.

The cries of protest from the black-coated undertakers gave him a momentary thrill of satisfaction.

And then he tore off down the road as if his life depended on it.

★ ★ ★

'Fee, did he do it? Did he really murder Poppy?'

Fee's best friend, Scarlett, jiggled from one foot to the other.

'Is that why he's disappeared?' Mandy added. 'Will the police find him? Go on, Fee – you must know something!'

Fee slammed her lunch tray down on the trolley.

'I haven't a clue!' she retorted, squashing her drinks can and dumping it in the bin. 'And frankly, I don't really care!'

Right now, the whereabouts of Bradley French was the last thing on her mind. The way her mates went on, you'd think the guy actually existed.

'But your dad must know!' Verity urged. 'Why can't you ask him?'

'Because,' shouted Fee, the last vestiges of her patience evaporating, 'some of us have more important things to worry about than some stupid soap, OK? Now just leave it, can't you?'

'Oh, get you!' muttered Tanya. 'PMT or what?'

I wish, thought Fee, pushing her way out of the cafeteria and heading down the corridor to the girls' toilets. But she had had twinges that morning, and maybe, just maybe...

'Hey, Fiona, what's going to happen to Bradley...?' Some over-eager little Year Eight grabbed her sleeve as she went past. She shrugged her off and didn't even bother replying.

Not for the first time, she wished she had normal parents doing normal jobs in a quiet and unembarrassing way. It was bad enough having a father who was on TV four times a week, flaunting himself as Bradley French, the womanising, double-dealing star of *Fiddler's Wharf*. But on top of that, she had to deal with her mother.

'Your mum is something else!' Scarlett had grinned the first time she'd met her. At least you couldn't fault her for accuracy, Fee thought dryly, dodging the gaggle of girls sharing lippy in front of the mirrors, and slipping into the first free toilet cubicle.

Scarlett, of course, meant it as a compliment; but then Scarlett had only seen the public side of Fee's mother. She didn't have to live with her.

'Why are you so horrible to your mum?' Scarlett had asked a couple of months earlier when she had been round at Fee's house.

'Me? Horrible to her?' Fee had protested. 'Didn't you hear what she said about me?'

Scarlett had sighed and inspected her fingernails.

'Well,' she had replied hesitatingly, 'she only said it because she cares.'

'Oh sure!' Fee had retorted sarcastically. 'What was it? If only Fiona would do something with her hair, her figure, her skin, her dress sense, the way she breathes in and out . . . dead caring, I call that!'

'Don't exaggerate!' Scarlett had admonished her. 'She just said that you could be really stunning if you made an effort. And you could!'

'Don't you start!' Fee had snapped back. 'You're supposed to be my mate.'

Of course, thought Fee now, leaning against the cubicle wall and not daring to slip down her panties because of what she might not find, it was her mother's job to be hypercritical of the entire universe. People in the public eye actually paid good money for her to slag them off and then set about changing everything about them. Image consultancy, it was called, and her mother was made for the role.

'Image is everything, Fiona,' she would sigh at least twice a week. 'First impressions are vital – and frankly, you're not sending out the right messages, sweetheart.'

Why her mother called her sweetheart, Fee didn't understand. She was pretty sure she didn't really like her much, not deep down; she was, after all, the afterthought, the baby born when Louise was already nine years old, the kid her mother never really wanted.

And now she was the teenager who still didn't fit the bill or fulfill any of her mother's dreams. Fee had always been a tomboy, always preferred dungarees and sweatshirts to the designer label kids' gear that her mother insisted on. She had hated the obligatory ballet classes and piano lessons and had been much happier playing with her worm farm, climbing trees or collecting snails from the rockery and racing them along her parents' handmade garden furniture. And even now, years after the activities of the insect world had ceased to hold any fascination for her, she was still a source of despair to her mother.

'It wasn't me that wanted another child, if you remember!' How many times had she heard her mother mutter those words to her father, usually when they were in the middle of one of their interminable rows, many of which started because of something Fee had or hadn't done.

'If you'd listened to me and sent her to a decent boarding school instead of that awful comprehensive, she'd have done just fine!' This was her father's stock reply, his way of absolving himself from any responsibility for what they called 'the way Fiona's turning out'.

'Why can't she be more like Louise?' When her mother got to that bit of the conversation, Fee always stopped eavesdropping and blocked her ears. She could have recited the words from memory: Louise is so attractive, lovely dress sense, always mixed with a nice type, never caused a moment's worry. It was hardly surprising, Fee thought, since precious Louise didn't have an original thought in her head and had always said and done everything her mother programmed her to. Child model, first class pianist, star of her snooty finishing school . . . Fee thought she would rather die than be like her sister. Luckily, Louise was working in New York now; three thousand miles was about the nearest Fee wanted to be to her oh-so-perfect sister.

'Hurry up in there! The other loo's bust!'

Fee's thoughts were interrupted by an agitated banging on the door.

'Won't be a minute!'

Slowly, with her eyes half closed, she slipped off her panties. Nothing. Not the merest stain. Instinctively, she rubbed her hand across her stomach, willing the familiar dull ache she had been sure she felt in Geography to return.

The only thing that was happening in her stomach was the churning of a whole load of over-active butterflies.

She bit her lip in an attempt to quell the sense of rising panic. Her heart racing, she grabbed her mobile phone from her pocket and flipped open the cover, flushing the loo with one hand and scrolling through to *MESSAGES* with the other.

'Please God,' she begged silently, 'let there be a message from Dean. Please.'

Hardly daring to breathe, she glanced at the screen. God was clearly preoccupied.

There was nothing. No text message, no voicemail.

Four days and not a single word. And she knew why. She'd messed up. It was because of what she'd told him on Sunday, she just knew it was. He'd got the hump and decided she was just too much of a kid for someone like him.

'Are you OK in there?' More thumping on the door.

Fee slipped her phone in her pocket and opened the door. Verity Fisher was hopping from one foot to the other, looking decidedly irritated.

'About time!' she hissed. 'Have you got a you-know-what? The machine's empty and my period's come early!'

Lucky you, thought Fee, putting her hand in her pocket and fingering the slightly squashed Tampax that had been there for days. Perhaps, sod's law being what it was, if she gave it to Verity, her own period would come that afternoon.

'Thanks, you saved my life!' Verity grinned, grabbing

the tampon and slamming the cubicle door. 'Hey, you are coming to the Fair tomorrow night, aren't you? There's a whole gang of us going and guess what? Warren said he'll come . . . he is so gorgeous . . . '

Fee wasn't in the mood to hang about and listen to the saga of Verity's latest love affair. As she ambled up the corridor, she began doing mental arithmetic in her head – for the fifth time that week. Maybe she'd got it wrong. Maybe her maths was all over the place.

But she knew it wasn't.

The answer always came out the same.

'Hey, Fee! Wait for me!'

She couldn't mistake Scarlett's strident tones pursuing her up the corridor.

'Are you OK?' she asked. 'You were in a right state earlier – what's up?'

'I'm late,' Fee said flatly.

'Oh, Miss Perry won't care!' Scarlett slipped an arm through Fee's. 'Just smile sweetly and say—'

'I don't mean late for English,' Fee interjected. 'Late. Overdue.'

A look of recognition flitted across Scarlett's face.

'Oh, I get it! Poor you – I get so moody if I'm a day or two late. I'll explain to the others—'

'No you don't get it!' To her horror, Fee felt her eyes fill with tears and she turned away in a desperate attempt to compose herself. 'Scar, I—'

She couldn't say the words. If she didn't say them, they wouldn't come true. And she'd had that pain this morning.

And she was pretty sure she could feel it coming back.

'You don't mean...?' Scarlett stopped dead in her tracks, causing a couple of Year Nines to career into the back of her. 'But you and Dean – you haven't... have you?'

'Ssshh! Keep your voice down!' Fee muttered as they reached the corridor to the English block, avoiding the need to answer Scarlett's question directly and make herself seem a total idiot. 'Anyway, I'm sure it'll be OK – I've had twinges off and on all day.'

'That's a good sign,' Scarlett acknowledged. 'Perhaps it was just going to Greece on holiday that did it – my mum always misses when she goes abroad.'

'She does?' Fee's heart lifted. She'd never thought of that.

'Look, I must dash,' said Scarlett. 'Dentist, worse luck! Keep me posted, yeah?'

'I will – and thanks!'

It was going to be OK. Any day now it would come and everything would be back to normal.

Except that Dean hadn't phoned for four whole days.

If he didn't call tonight, she would have to go looking for him. The problem was that she didn't have a clue where to start.

2

'Do you want some help, Miss?'

Jay knew that he wasn't doing himself any favours; he could already hear the derisory titters from the stragglers leaving the classroom. But he reckoned he had no choice. The next ten minutes or so would be the dodgy time; now that the end-of-school bell had rung, Rick would be looking for him – and Jay knew that if he wanted his facial bones to remain intact, he had to make sure Rick didn't get to him. If being labelled a teacher's pet was the price he had to pay – well, he guessed it was worth it.

'Thank you, Jay!' Miss Perry smiled at him and thrust a pile of folders into his arms. 'I don't suppose you could help me get this lot to my car?'

''Course, Miss!'

It wasn't that he wanted to hang about; he would far rather have dashed home to check on Nan. Well, no; that wasn't really true. To be honest, going home was the one thing he dreaded, especially today. That business with the sandwich; surely it meant his grandmother was losing it big time? He didn't get it; he could understand why she put lemonade down the toilet instead of bleach, or tried to put the milk in the airing cupboard and the laundry in the fridge. They were the sort of mistakes anyone could make if they were in a rush. And Nan was always rushing. But the sandwich ...

His eyes darted from left to right as he followed Miss Perry down the long corridor and out into the school forecourt. No sign of Rick or Matt. So far so good.

'It's good of you to help me out, Jay.' Miss Perry paused to catch her breath and turned to face him. 'I was wanting to have a word.'

'Yes, Miss?' Jay avoided her gaze and edged forward towards the staff car park. Standing in full view of everyone, chatting to a teacher, was not exactly the best tactical move.

'You are three days late handing in your English assignment,' she said sternly. 'It's not a good start to the school year.'

Jay sighed inwardly.

'Sorry, Miss,' he muttered. 'I'll bring it tomorrow.'

'Good,' replied Miss Perry with a satisfied nod. 'You can't afford to get lax this close to your GCSEs – especially since you're going to be taking English in the Sixth Form.'

Oh sure, Jay muttered under his breath. Like that's really going to happen.

'Say again?'

Miss Perry glanced at him enquiringly.

'I'll bring it,' Jay repeated, stifling a sigh at the thought of the hours of work ahead. It wasn't that he didn't enjoy English – he did. Just like he enjoyed History and French – most things, actually, except PE and sport. But by the time he'd got home and cooked supper – Nan had gone off cooking and would have lived on jam sandwiches and ice cream if he hadn't put his foot down – and then washed

up and sorted the washing, and scooted round to the Open
Til Late store, and found all the things his grandmother
had lost during the day, and ironed his shirt for the next
morning, he was so tired he couldn't concentrate on the
TV, never mind an in-depth analysis of *To Kill a Mocking
Bird*.

'I know I can rely on you really,' beamed Miss Perry, the
way teachers always did once they thought they'd got their
own way. 'Oh, and don't forget that tomorrow is the last
day for bringing your form back too.'

'Form, Miss?'

He knew quite well what she was on about, but he
needed time to work out his reply.

'For the French exchange, Jay!' she sighed a little
impatiently. 'Mr Sinclair was only saying today that he still
has to place you with a family, and he can't do that until . . .'

'I'm not going, Miss.'

'Not going?' His year tutor looked gobsmacked. 'Of
course you're—'

'No, Miss. I can't. Sorry.'

'But Jason, why?'

He shrugged.

'France costs a lot, Miss.'

That should do it, he thought.

Miss Perry's face flushed.

'Oh Jay, I'm sorry. Thoughtless of me. But not to
worry . . .'

She'd bought it. Ace. Normally, he would have done
anything to hide the fact that they were hard up; and

besides, if he'd really wanted to go he could have managed it, what with his paper round, and his Saturday job at the dry cleaners and the bit of money in his Building Society. But there was no way he could go. He'd learned his lesson the last time, on the field trip to Wales. And besides, how could he invite some French guy back to his house?

'. . . because The Foundation Fund can cough up the money.'

'No, Miss!'

Why couldn't she just accept it and drop the subject?

'Jay, it's OK. It's there for just this sort of thing – supporting talented pupils who can't . . . well, who don't feel able to meet the cost themselves. Now look, I must dash, but just you get that form back to Mr Sinclair and the school will sort out the rest.'

Terrific, thought Jay. Try to avoid one problem and you get lumbered with another.

'That's settled then!' she cried, and Jay didn't have the energy to argue with her. He'd just have to think up some other good excuse by tomorrow.

'Here we are!' Miss Perry gestured towards her Ford Fiesta. 'If you can just dump those books on . . .'

Jay didn't catch the end of her sentence. He was staring at two figures lolling against the wall by the main exit.

Rick and Matt shoved their hands in their pockets and began, very slowly, to move in his direction.

'Could I cadge a lift, Miss?'

It was a long shot, but he had to do something.

'A lift?'

Miss Perry was frowning at him.

'Please, Miss.' His mouth was so dry that he could hardly get the words out.

'Jay, I go in the opposite direction to you,' she said. 'And anyway, you know it's against school rules – it's not appropriate for me to . . .'

She was already in the driving seat, pulling her seat belt across her stomach and averting her gaze.

'Anyway,' she added brightly, slotting the key into the ignition and firing the engine, 'what was the Head telling us all in assembly? More exercise means more energy! The walk will do you good!'

She slammed the door of the car shut and raised her hand in a wave.

'Don't forget; one essay, one form!'

Her tyres squealed slightly on the loose gravel as she swung her car out of the gates and into the main road.

From the corner of his eye, he could see Rick and Matt swaggering towards him.

There was only one thing for it.

He turned and belted back towards the school building. He couldn't spare the time, Nan would start fretting, but frankly she'd have to fret for once. There'd be a lot more to worry about if Rick and Matt duffed him up.

'Hey, watch it!' Fiona Bayliss sidestepped as he careered straight into her. 'Oh – it's you!'

He would have liked it if she had sounded a bit more enthusiastic.

'Sorry,' he gabbled. 'Forgot something – sorry.'

She hitched her bag onto her left shoulder and gave a half smile.

'It's OK,' she said. 'I was miles away too! Oh, and I'm sorry too – about lunch time.'

'Lunch time?'

'Science Club,' she went on. 'I was – well, I felt sick so I didn't go.'

'That's OK, I missed it too,' he confessed. 'I had to—'

'Oh yeah – your gran! Is everything OK?'

That's what he hated. Everyone knowing that he'd been called home; having to make up excuses all the time. He wished the secretary had been a bit more discreet.

'Sure!' he said, trying to sound as blasé as possible. 'I'd left my essay at home and she knew I'd be for it with Miss Perry.'

'Wow!' Fiona raised an eyebrow. 'She's on the ball!'

The irony of her comment cut through him like a knife.

'Anyway,' she went on hurriedly, 'got to go. See you!'

'Wait!' He swallowed hard. 'I was wondering whether...'

'What?'

'Whether you'd... I mean, when shall we finish the competition entry?'

No point asking her to go to the Fair. What would a girl like her want to do with someone like him?

She shrugged her shoulders and started walking away.

'Whenever,' she said wearily. 'Reena's still off sick, so we'll sort it when she gets back, OK?'

He turned to follow her but in an instant, Rick was

blocking his way, Matt close on his heels. He had no choice but to stop.

'So, Squirt . . . ?'

'Don't call me that!'

'I'll call you,' said Rick, slowly enunciating every word, 'whatever I damn like.'

Jay clenched his teeth, turned and tried to dodge past them, but Rick grabbed his arm.

'I wasn't happy with what you did at lunch time,' said Rick, pulling a piece of gum lodged in the corner of his mouth. 'And I want compensation!'

He smiled triumphantly as he said the last word.

'£5 should do it, right, Matt?' He turned to his mate for approval.

'£10, I reckon, Rick,' drawled Matt. 'Fiver for you, fiver for me.'

Jay's heart lurched.

'You can't do that . . . !' As he said the words, Jay realised his mistake.

Rick took a step closer, so close that Jay could smell his foul breath and the odour from his armpits.

'I can do whatever I like, Midget! Get the money. Or else . . .'

And with that, he gave Jay a shove, turned and strode off with Matt.

Jay stood stock still in the playground. For several minutes, he didn't move. There was no need. Wherever he went, and whatever he did, there was going to be trouble.

Rick and Matt would see to that.

He wished that he could stop time right then. Before all the bad things started to pile up and bury him.

★ ★ ★

Lyall stood in the doorway to the Senior Art Studio and took a long, deep breath. This was better; this was worth making the effort to come back into school. He felt an OK person here. For one thing, the Art block was set apart from the main school and felt like another place entirely – his sort of place. He loved the aroma of oil paint mixed with moist clay and he loved the mess – the paint smeared table tops, the piles of brushes and jars in the old-fashioned sinks and the fact that two of the paintings lining the mustard-coloured walls were his.

He wasn't good at very much in life, he thought to himself, shrugging his arms out of his blazer and slinging it across the back of a chair. Maths and Science made no sense to him, and he found Geography a complete waste of time. He liked poetry, but of course, no one in their right mind would admit to something like that. But Art – that was OK; cool, even. People admired artists. And you could lose yourself in painting and sculpture – make something that was all your own, full of all your feelings but with no rules and regulations; a bit like poetry really except that you didn't have to worry about spelling the words wrongly.

Of course, he wasn't meant to be here. The end of school bell had gone ten minutes ago, and he was meant to be waiting outside the staff room, just so that Mr Willoughby could have a go at him yet again. Well, stuff that.

If he went, he'd get angry. And getting angry was the one thing he had to avoid. He was doing well; so well that the behavioural therapist guy said he only had to go once a month from now on. He wasn't going to let Mr Willoughby mess his head up. No way.

He thought back to the beginning of the afternoon, when he'd just made it to Registration, sweaty and out of breath from running.

'Lyall Porter?' His Head of Year had actually been calling his name as Lyall crashed through the door.

'Here, Sir!' Lyall had gasped, and instantly noted the fleeting expression of surprise that flashed across Mr Willoughby's ruddy features.

'Oh – so you've decided to turn up, have you, Lyall?'

'It would appear so, Sir.'

Lyall had glanced down at his body as if to check its presence, and then grinned as muffled titters spread around the class. He was almost as good at making people laugh as he was at painting pictures.

'Nice one!' someone had murmured appreciatively. Mr Willoughby, however, seemed immune to humour.

'But you weren't here this morning, were you?' he had demanded, tapping his pen on the table and glaring at Lyall. 'Or yesterday, if I recall.'

'No, Sir.'

'And why was that, Lyall?'

'I was sick, Sir.'

Mr Willoughby had sniffed, whether from disbelief or annoyance at a valid excuse for his absence, Lyall hadn't been quite sure. For a moment, he had felt the usual pang of guilt at his lie; but then, he had rationalised quickly to himself, it wasn't a total lie, was it? OK, so after that one time, he hadn't actually thrown up any more, but he'd been sick; sick to the pit of his stomach at what he'd overheard Maddy and Patrick talking about; sick with fear if he was honest.

The fear of being left again. Like before. And of messing up again. Like before.

'Sick, were you, Lyall?'

The expression on Mr Willoughby's face had caused Lyall's stomach to lurch dangerously.

'Funny that,' the tutor had remarked. 'We phoned your home this morning and were told that you had left for school in the usual way. Explain!'

'I thought I was getting better, but then I was sick on the way to school, Sir.'

Lyall had held the tutor's gaze, knowing that eye contact counted for a lot with teachers.

'And so I turned round and went back – but by then my... everyone had left for work.'

Clever one, Lyall. You're doing good. He had repeated the phrases over and over in his head – positive strokes, his therapist called them.

For a long moment, Mr Willoughby had said nothing. Then he had snatched up the register and flipped the page.

'Melanie Reilly, Russell Stern, Adam Swinley...'

Mr Willoughby had stormed his way to the end of Registration, slammed the register shut and stood up.

'Right! To your lessons, everyone, and be quick about it!'

He had clearly been in a bad mood. But that was OK – Lyall knew about bad moods and he guessed that it couldn't be much fun being cooped up in school all day, sniffing your own BO and trying to make Geography sound interesting.

'And you, Lyall Porter...'

Mr Willoughby had paused in the doorway, and a cluster of kids had backed up behind him.

'Me, Sir?'

'Yes, you, Lyall!' Mr Willoughby had stepped to one side and gestured to the rest of the class to move on. 'According to your mother...'

'Foster mother!' He would never have bothered correcting anyone in the past – but that was before yesterday.

'Yes, well...' For a moment, Mr Willoughby had seemed fazed. 'Whatever. Anyway, she told me that you weren't ill at home yesterday either. You left at the normal time. So I think you and I have a bit of talking to do, don't you?'

Lyall said nothing. That's what they'd told him to do when he started to feel angry – just keep quiet and think of other things.

'I'll see you after school – 3.45 outside the staff room,' Mr Willoughby had insisted. 'Now get along to your lesson!'

'Sir.'

Good man, Lyall. Nice response. Respectful. Same time next week?

The words of his therapist echoing in his head, he had managed to walk away without even clenching his fists.

Now, fingering a lump of moist clay and staring out of the window onto the games field, he wondered just what Maddy had said to Mr Willoughby on the telephone. Had she told him what they were planning, her and Patrick? No, probably not; after all, they hadn't had the guts to say anything even to him yet. And he had been too scared to ask. But tonight . . .

'Good heavens, Lyall, what's that bit of clay ever done to you?'

It wasn't until Mrs Faber's jocular tones interrupted his thoughts that he realised that he was pounding the clay rhythmically with his left fist.

'I was just . . .'

Lyall jumped to his feet, shoved the clay to one side and grabbed his blazer.

'Hang on a jiffy!' Mrs Faber called after him. 'Have you got a spare few minutes?'

Lyall hesitated. He'd assumed that Mr Willoughby had sent her to look for him but she was smiling broadly which suggested she hadn't a clue that he was meant to be somewhere else.

'Only I'd like to talk to you about an idea I had,' she went on, perching her ample bottom on the edge of the nearest table and pulling out a chair.

'For your GCSE,' she added, patting the chair and gesturing him to sit down.

Lyall could feel the grin spreading across his face. This was cool. The perfect alibi.

'Sorry, Mr Willoughby, but I had to talk to Mrs Faber about my work.'

He couldn't moan at that, could he? Not when he'd spent half the term telling Lyall to get a grip and knuckle down and make something of himself before it was too late.

'I mean, if you've got to dash home...' Mrs Faber began.

Home? No way.

'No, it's fine,' he said, sitting down. 'What was it?'

'Sculpture,' she said decisively. 'That's going to be the second string to your bow.'

'Miss?'

She was a nice enough woman, Mrs Faber, but she did come out with some weird things at times.

'I was very impressed by your work last year,' she went on. 'I know you are happy taking Art, but now that we're a City Academy, we can offer you GCSE Sculpture as well.'

Lyall's eyes widened. Normally teachers were telling him what he couldn't do, not offering him more.

'I think you'd enjoy it, Lyall,' she went on earnestly. 'It would build on the three dimensional work we've been doing in Art – but give you far more scope and...'

'But I've never done any sculpture, Miss!' he protested.

'Oh, Lyall, really!' She waved a hand dismissively. 'I've

never eaten sushi, but that won't stop me going to a Japanese restaurant with my friends tonight. Experimentation, Lyall – exploration! It's what life is all about!'

Oh sure, he thought. Life was about keeping your head down and then thinking up stonking good excuses when you messed up.

'But, Miss, what if I can't do it?' He wasn't about to set himself up to fail again – it was bad enough having been kept back a year when he was fourteen and taking his GCSEs later than all his old mates.

'Listen to me, Lyall,' Mrs Faber went on. 'You've had a tough time, one way and another. I know you find a lot of subjects tricky...'

A snort escaped from Lyall's nostrils. Tricky? Well, that was one way to put it, he guessed.

'...but art is something you have a real flair for. Your painting is excellent, it's full of perception and passion and emotion. But it's not good simply to stick with what's safe – you want to stretch yourself, take up a new challenge.'

She grinned at him.

'And you're good enough to do the whole course in one year!'

Lyall stared at her. No one ever said he was good enough at anything. Ever.

'But, Miss, what would I make?'

'Sculpt, Lyall, sculpt. You make cakes, you sculpt figures!'

She picked up a pile of dirty palettes and dumped them in the sink.

'You can create whatever you like – a self portrait, maybe? No, you did that for one of your paintings and very good it was too. But we need variety.'

She paused and then snapped her fingers.

'Got it!'

She opened her handbag and took out a key, unlocked one of the metal cabinets and handed him a camera.

'There!' she said. 'I can't spare it for long, I'm afraid, but you can use it for a few days. Snap away at anyone you see; capture the faces, the expressions – and then use the pictures to inspire your sculpting.'

Lyall stared first at the camera in his hand, and then at Mrs Faber.

'You mean – you're going to let me use this?' He enunciated each word carefully, just to make sure that he hadn't got the wrong end of the stick. He did that quite often and it always landed him in deep trouble.

'That's right!' she agreed cheerfully. 'I know you'll take good care of it. The instruction book is in the carrying case. Oh, and if you need more film, just ask!'

She grabbed her bag and fished out a leaflet.

'Take this,' she said, thrusting it into his hands. 'It gives you some idea of what the course is all about.'

Lyall scanned the sheet.

'. . . preparation and sketch book work using 2D skills . . . techniques of 3D work . . . ceramic skills . . . plaster/ mod.roc work . . .'

He raised his eyes briefly and blushed.

'What does it all mean, Miss?'

'It means a lot of hard work – and heaps of fun!' she trilled cheerfully. 'Now, I must dash – think about it, Lyall, and we'll talk some more!'

She snatched up a pile of sketches and kicked the double doors open with her foot.

'Wait, Miss!' He hadn't meant to say anything but as she paused, half out of the door, and turned back to face him, he knew he had to tell her.

'I was meant to see Mr Willoughby, Miss. At quarter to four.' He took a deep breath. 'Only I didn't want . . .'

He stopped. How could he explain? If he said he'd skived off school, she'd take the camera away; the school had this thing about privileges being removed when responsibilities are ignored. They even had it written in huge letters on every notice board in the place.

'That is, I didn't want to tell him the real . . .'

Oh, what was the point? Whatever he said, he was in trouble. Why the hell hadn't he kept his mouth shut?

Mrs Faber held his gaze for the briefest moment.

'Well, dear me – I'll have to apologise to Mr Willoughby for keeping you so long, won't I?' she said. 'Not that he'll mind – not with you about to become one of the first Bishop Andrew students to sit the GCSE Sculpture.'

She winked at him. That's when it dawned on him. She was going to take the blame – say it was her fault he never turned up at the staff room. She was on his side. No, that couldn't be right; teachers weren't like that. They watched one another's backs all the time.

'Lyall – it's OK.'

She said it so calmly and look so unruffled that he believed her.

'Now get off home and read that leaflet!' she laughed. 'Or it will be me that's in trouble for missing the staff meeting!'

For a while he just stood there, listening to the clatter of her heels as she ran down the stairs.

Then he turned back into the studio and picked up the camera.

He walked over to the window and held the viewfinder to his eye. Everything was blurred and out of focus. He scrabbled in the carrying case, found the manual and began fiddling with the settings.

You could do anything. Zoom in, zoom out – turn things on their side, even take pictures of yourself once you'd worked out the timer switch.

'Yes!' Lyall punched the air with his fist. This was ace. This was something else.

She thought he was good. Good. He savoured the word, whispering it under his breath.

He couldn't wait to show Maddy and Patrick – they'd be dead chuffed and...

Then he remembered. They probably wouldn't be chuffed at all. After all, they didn't give a damn about him any more, did they?

They were too busy making plans for dumping him.

Well, see if he cared. He'd show them; he'd damn well cheer when they finally got round to telling him.

But he did care. He cared more than he would ever have dreamed.

He didn't know why. He'd been in enough places in his life, one more wouldn't matter.

It was just that Maddy and Patrick – well, he felt different about them.

He kind of liked them. Not loved them, of course. He'd never love anyone else ever again. No way.

But he liked them.

He also hated them like hell.

* * *

Fee knew she shouldn't give in to the urge for chocolate, but her relief at Scarlett's explanation of her overdue period had kicked her appetite into overdrive, and besides, she consoled herself, she did deserve a reward; she'd been really strong for two whole weeks. She'd lost four pounds already. Sadly she had another eleven to go.

She hadn't always been plump. There were photos at home of her as a little kid, skinny and lanky, with short curly hair and huge eyes. 'My little Bambi' her father used to call her. She was still the tallest girl in her class, but now her unruly hair was way below her broad shoulders, she needed a 38DD bra and she yearned to have one of those tight little bottoms that looked so good in hipster jeans. Most of the boys she'd been out with had only hung around for a few weeks, and the girls they'd ended up with had all been petite and sexy looking. Each time, she'd vowed that she would lose weight; each time the diet lasted a few days and then she lost interest.

And then she'd met Dean.

She smiled to herself as she tossed chocolate bars into her wire basket, remembering the day when he'd walked into *Pete's Aaaaah!*, the new pizzeria where she'd just got a holiday job for the summer. She wasn't the only waitress who had stopped dead in her tracks at the sight of him. He was even taller than her, with floppy blond hair, a mahogany sun tan and angular features. As he pulled off his shades and scanned the crowded room for a table, his eyes had alighted on Fee.

'Hi, babes! Got a table free?'

She had felt herself blushing as he winked at her.

'Smoking or non smoking?' The words had come out as a high-pitched squeak.

'Whichever keeps me close to you!' He had grinned at her, his piercing blue eyes not leaving her face. 'I'm very flexible!'

All her allotted tables had been full.

'Hang on a minute!' she had said, rushing across to a family of three who were lingering over a cup of coffee and slapping their bill down in front of them. Just go, she willed them silently. Please, just go.

Of course, they hadn't. The kid had wanted another Pepsi, and the mother decided to make a phone call from her mobile. Dean had ended up on Lisa's table and she'd flirted with him the whole way through his meal.

But to her amazement, he'd lingered by the door when he'd finished, and beckoned to her. She knew she'd catch it from Casey, the up-herself manageress, but she'd slipped out into the street anyway.

'Was everything OK?' She hadn't been able to think of anything more intelligent to say.

'No!' He pulled a face. 'You weren't there to look after me.'

'You look quite capable of looking after yourself,' she had grinned, pleased to have engaged her brain enough for a slightly more sophisticated conversation.

'So what time do you get off?' he had asked. 'Hopefully – with me!'

The innuendo wasn't lost on her, and she felt her heart rate increase to life-threatening proportions.

'Five o'clock,' she had stammered.

'See you at The Melting Pot at eight, then!' It wasn't a question. He had just grinned, waved and strode off down the street without a backward glance.

And that had been the start of it. The best seven weeks of her life.

Until last weekend.

Why had she said what she'd said? she thought miserably, standing in line at the checkout. Why had she been so dumb? She could have kept it a secret for a bit longer, and they could have gone on as before.

But now she couldn't take the words back – and he had got fed up with her, she just knew he had.

She walked out into the September sunshine, peeling back the wrapper from a Twix bar and watching as a couple of guys pasted Town Fair posters to a lamppost upside down. They'd been planning to go to the Fair, her and Dean; it was going to be bigger than ever this year, what with it being eight hundred years since King someone or other gave a Royal Charter to the borough. Dean loved roller coasters and even though she was scared stiff of them, she could have buried her head in his shoulder and he'd have hugged her tight.

She shook herself out of her reverie. She couldn't bear the thought of it being over – and now, what if her period didn't come, what if she was . . . ?

'Hey, Fee! Wait for us!'

Scarlett's strident tones were unmistakable. Fee turned, a half smile on her face, a smile which faded somewhat rapidly when she realised that Tanya was only a couple of steps behind.

'You were miles away!' Scarlett remarked accusingly. 'We called you three times.'

'Dreaming of lover boy, were you?' teased Tanya.

'Shut up, Tanya!' Scarlett coloured as she scowled at her mate.

Fee glared at Scarlett.

'You promised . . .' she began.

'Sorry – it just slipped out.' Scarlett had the good grace to look embarrassed.

Fee's heart sank. If Motormouth Tanya knew about Dean, soon the entire year would be in on it. And if Dean had dumped her, she'd just look a complete fool.

'What's the big secret anyway?' Tanya demanded. 'Shock, horror! Fee's sixteen and she's finally got a boyfriend!'

'Shut it, Tanya!' Scarlett snapped. 'Fee's a very private person.'

Fee smiled wanly, knowing from Scarlett's quick wink and imperceptible shake of the head, that she hadn't told Tanya all the details. Nevertheless, Fee wondered not for the first time whether letting Scarlett in on her secret had been the best idea. She hadn't been exactly enthusiastic when Fee had phoned her at eight o'clock on the Sunday morning after that first date, simply because she couldn't wait to tell someone.

'He's gorgeous!' she'd enthused down the phone. 'I've never met anyone like him. He's so much more sophisticated than guys our age.'

She was willing Scarlett to ask how old he was, and she did.

'Twenty-two!' Fee had breathed triumphantly. 'He's so mature . . .'

'Fee, are you mad?' Scarlett had sounded anything but impressed. 'If a guy his age is interested in someone of sixteen, he wants only one thing.'

'He's not like that!' Fee had burst out.

'They're all like that!' Scarlett had retorted.

They'd had words after that. OK, not words – a full blown argument that had gone on for days. Fee told Scarlett she had no experience – after all, she'd been with Sam since they were both thirteen. Scarlett told Fee that at least she knew all there was to know about Sam and how did she know that Dean wasn't on the run from the police, or married with a kid? Fee accused Scarlett of being a drama queen, and Scarlett demanded that Fee introduce her to Dean.

'I'm good at sizing up guys,' she had declared. 'I'll be able to tell where he's really coming from.'

Of course, Fee had stamped on that idea at once. If Scarlett met Dean, he would suss that Fee had lied to him – and she couldn't risk that. Not yet.

'He's going away for a couple of weeks,' she had lied hastily. 'I'll sort it once he gets back.'

She knew Scarlett would be on holiday herself by then.

'Well, promise me you'll be careful?' Scarlett had urged her, the night before she left for Tunisia with Sam and his parents.

'Promise me you won't tell anyone – not yet?' Fee had pleaded back.

They'd both promised. And, thought Fee wryly, starting to edge away up the street, they'd both broken their promises.

'Anyway,' Tanya went on, falling in step beside her, 'I guess you've got more on your mind now than mystery boy! We know now why you were so off with us at lunch time.'

Fee stopped dead in her tracks.

'You didn't . . . ?' She turned to Scarlett, the sentence hanging unfinished in the air.

'Of course I didn't!' Scarlett hissed back.

'Have a Rolo?' Fee thrust the tube at her friends. Tanya grabbed one, but Scarlett shook her head.

'But you should have told us, Fee,' she stressed. 'I mean,

I know you're probably dead embarrassed and everything but—'

'We're supposed to be your mates!' Tanya interjected.

'Told you what? What are you on about?' Fee demanded.

Scarlett glanced at Tanya and said nothing. She simply stepped to one side and pointed across the street, to where a newsvendor was standing, clutching copies of the local evening paper.

'SOAP STAR IN STREET BRAWL!'

The six-inch high letters on the billboard screamed out at Fee.

Tanya pulled a copy of the *Chronicle* from her school bag and shoved into Fee's hands.

Fee stared at the photograph on the front page.

A man, fist raised and teeth gritted, was glowering straight at the camera. Behind him, a crowd of people were standing, wide-eyed with alarm.

'Fisticuffs in Fulham!' cried the caption.

'Is it true? All the things they're saying in the paper?' Tanya demanded.

Fee didn't reply. She didn't know what to say. Because the man staring at the camera was her father.

And he wasn't even supposed to be in Fulham.

He was supposed to be filming in Spain.

3

The dented Coke can bounced off the side of the bus shelter and into the path of a passing taxi. Jay watched with a degree of satisfaction as it was flattened under the wheels. Pity it was just a dumb drinks can and not Rick bloody Barnes.

He caught sight of his reflection in the grimy perspex frame covering the bus timetable, and turned away in irritation. Why was he such a weed? He'd always been puny and as a little kid, always the one off sick from school. He'd started his primary school three weeks after everyone else because he'd had his appendix out and almost every term, even when his asthma wasn't playing up, he'd had long absences with throat infections and stomach upsets. The doctors had said he'd grow out of it, but after just three days at Bishop Andrew, he'd got glandular fever and that had been that.

By the time he went back, everyone had got mates of their own, and even though his health was OK now, he'd hovered on the edges ever since. He knew it was his own fault; for one thing, he was useless at sport and for another, he was clever. The first he couldn't do anything about but the second, he reckoned he'd got sussed. He just kept his head down, never answered questions more often that he had to and always made sure that his work wasn't perfect. OK, so the teachers nagged him about falling standards and wasting a brain, but at least he didn't get called a swot. It was no skin off his nose; he couldn't go to uni anyway, not with Nan like she was, so why make life hard for himself?

It was a strategy that had worked with most of his classmates, he reflected as he mooched down the street, his hands stuffed into his jacket pocket. The ones that didn't ignore him totally, tolerated him. Some, like Fiona, even chatted to him now and again. But not Rick. Rick hated him. Rick was out for his blood.

And Jay hadn't a clue why.

And now he and Matt wanted money. He knew he would be dumb to give it to them – but he knew that the consequences of refusing were too horrible to contemplate. And it was Thursday. His paper-round money would be due tomorrow; if he could just persuade the Patels to give it to him today instead, he would be able to give Rick his tenner.

After all, it would be just this once. He'd make damn sure that nothing like the sandwich incident ever happened again. They wouldn't have any reason to get at him again, not if he watched his step.

His mind made up, he crossed the road to the corner shop and pushed open the glass door.

'There! You see, I told you it was just a mistake!' Mrs Patel beamed at her grim-faced husband and clapped her hands in pleasure. 'Am I not always right?'

She turned to Jay and beamed.

'Don't you worry, it's easily done, easily done!'

Jay looked from her to her glowering husband and back

51

again. They were both watching him expectantly.

'Did I deliver something to the wrong house?' he asked anxiously, his heart sinking at the thought of anything that would stop them paying him a day early.

The smile faded from Mrs Patel's chubby face.

'Nothing wrong with the papers,' she said. 'I thought—'

'Only I've come about the money,' Jay rushed on, before she could continue. 'I know it's a day—'

'See?' Mrs Patel was all smiles again. 'I knew that Mrs Rust would realise what she'd done!'

At the sound of his grandmother's name, all thoughts of money went out of Jay's head.

'So — shall I just deduct the money from your pay, or have you brought it with you?'

Mr Patel was clearly determined to get down to basics.

'Let me see,' he muttered. 'What was it she took?'

'Took?' The word escaped from Jay's lips as a fractured whisper.

'Two magazines – that's £4.40 – then there was the fish paste and the marshmallow teacakes – that's another £2.05. That makes £6.45.'

Jay swallowed hard.

'She was in such a hurry, your granny,' murmured Mrs Patel soothingly. 'Easy to make a mistake – she'll have given you the money?'

She cocked her head to one side.

'Er – no,' Jay improvised hastily. 'She wanted to, but I said that I'd get you to take it out of my pay – save time!'

He tried to smile confidently.

'If that's OK with you,' he added.

Mr Patel shrugged.

'Doesn't matter to me either way,' he remarked. 'Just as long as I get paid.'

Mrs Patel struck a key on the cash register and the drawer sprang open.

'So,' she said. 'We owe you £8.50 so that means . . .'

She closed her eyes and did a quick calculation in her head.

'Just £2.05 for you!' She handed him the cash. 'You might as well take the papers for this evening with you now, OK?'

She thrust the bright yellow plastic sack in his arms.

'Oh, and say thank you to your granny for me!'

I'll say a lot more than that, thought Jay ruefully, pushing open the glass door and stepping into the street. What did she want with that stuff anyway? OK, so she liked to flick through a magazine in the evenings – but fish paste? Marshmallows?

He'd have to tell her. Sort her out. OK, old people got forgetful, he knew that – but she wasn't that old. Sixty-five last birthday – hardly geriatric.

He quickened his pace and crossed Kendal Street, breaking into a run as the first drops of rain began to fall. He'd have to get his nan to pay him back – there was no time to go to the bank and draw from his savings and if he turned up at school without the cash . . .

By the time he reached his house, he was panting for breath.

'There you are!'

His grandmother was standing at the foot of the stairs wearing one of her smart summer dresses and an old straw hat. On her feet were a pair of very ancient flip flops.

'Nan?' He dumped the paper sack on the floor.

'Good gracious, you took your time!' she exclaimed.

'I went to the paper shop and . . .'

'Now then, are you ready? Have you got your trunks? And your rubber ring? You know I won't let you into the water without that rubber ring.'

Keep calm, Jay told himself, taking a deep breath. It'll be fine.

'Nan, we're not going anywhere. Not right now. I've got my paper round to do, remember? How about I put the kettle on and then—'

'But we're going for our picnic!' cried Nan. 'I've got it all ready.'

She bent down and picked up her wicker shopping basket.

'Tea, squash, fish paste sandwiches . . .'

Jay laid a hand on her arm.

'Nan, listen. You didn't pay for—'

'You like fish paste, don't you? You've always liked fish paste – not like your mum, of course – she's the one for jam, jam and more jam . . .'

For a moment, Jay thought he would stop breathing. A band tightened round his chest and an image swam before his eyes. Sitting on a blue flowery lap and licking blackcurrant jam off long fingers, each with a sparkling ring on.

'One lick, two lick . . .'

He could hear the pretty, sing-song voice in his head.

'And I've got the chocolate marshmallows,' his grandmother was saying. 'Dreadful price, but after all it's a treat and—'

'You didn't pay for them!' Jay yelled at her, more angry because her words had shattered the fleeting memory than because of her empty-headedness. 'You just took them and I had to—'

'Of course I didn't pay! Never do – Mr Maxwell likes me to settle up at the end of the month.'

Mr Maxwell? Who the hell, he thought, was Mr Maxwell?

His grandmother gave him a gentle shove.

'So come on, love – get your rubber ring and let's be going. I told your mum we'd meet her at the Lido and . . .'

That did it. He couldn't take any more.

'Shut up, shut up, SHUT UP!' Jay snatched the basket from her hands and threw it to the floor. A couple of plastic beakers rolled dejectedly across the carpet.

'You're mad, you know that!' he shouted, and it was as if a great dam had just burst and all the things he'd thought and worried about for weeks on end came spilling out. 'Why can't you be normal? Why can't you be like you used to be?'

He paused, catching his breath.

'Temper, temper!' His nan waggled a finger at him. 'Bad-tempered little boys don't get taken to the Lido . . .'

'Stop it!' Jay shouted. 'The Lido's been shut for three years, Nan!'

He was half sobbing now.

'And Mum's dead! You know damn well she is – we go to the grave and put flowers on, remember?'

A veil passed over his grandmother's face.

'Dead. Barbara. Killed.'

There was no questioning in her voice. It was more as if she was trying to recall the items on a shopping list she'd mislaid.

She was staring at Jason.

'You scare me, you know that?' he shouted. 'You scare me rigid!'

He stopped, the anger ebbing from him as if someone had pulled a plug. She looked as if he had punched her in the face; she actually reeled back a step or two.

He was panting now, as heavily as if he had run all the way home from school without stopping. His nan stared at him, open-mouthed. And then, almost in slow motion, the corners of her mouth turned down, her chest heaved and a tear trickled down her cheek.

'I forgot – I thought . . . she's gone?'

'She died, remember,' he went on more softly. 'With Dad. In that car crash.'

'Car crash. Car crash.' She repeated the words, nodding slowly as she did so. Then suddenly her mood changed.

'No need to bring all that up again!' Nan's voice took on its normal timbre and became brisk and matter of fact. 'What's done is done!'

She took a deep breath and patted his shoulder.

'You're a good boy, Jay,' she said. 'Don't worry – we can always have a picnic another day.'

Jay didn't speak because he didn't know what to say. Something had clearly made her mind click back to reality and he wasn't about to say a single word that might start her off again.

He wouldn't even mention the shopping. It was paid for and that was that. He'd ask her for some cash later when things had calmed down.

'Make me a cup of tea, there's a good lad!' his nan asked. 'I'm parched!'

'OK!' He tried to sound cheerful, even whistling the odd snatch of a pop song as he plugged in the kettle.

But his stomach was churning and his eyes kept darting round the kitchen for signs of anything out of place.

'Had a good day, Jay?' His nan had plonked herself down on one of the kitchen chairs. 'Everything go all right?'

There was no point being honest.

'Yeah, Nan, fine thanks,' he lied. 'Just great. Who's Mr Maxwell, by the way?'

He hadn't meant to say anything. If it started her off again . . .

'Mr Maxwell? Good gracious, there's a blast from the past. Used to run the corner shop when your grampy and I were first married. Nice man – awful bad breath, though . . .'

And she was off. Jay didn't listen because he was too busy trying to fight the rising panic that was gripping him.

Nan had thought he was little again; she'd thought his

57

mother was still alive. And she'd imagined that the groceries came from a man who had a shop forty years ago.

She really was going mad.

And he hadn't a clue what he was meant to do about it.

★ ★ ★

Fee sat down on the grass, her back against the tree and watched the gangs of men erecting roller coasters and waltzers for the Town Fair. Despite the turmoil of her mind, she couldn't help smiling to herself as she remembered how her parents had gone ballistic when they realised that for five days every September, the view from their expensive new home would be wrecked with what her mother called 'trash and tack'.

'It will attract all the wrong types,' she had complained. 'The Belgate kids, all that sort.'

As far as her mother was concerned, Belgate was a definite no-go area, the worst possible part of Harpleton – but then, her mother thought anywhere that didn't have designer boutiques and café-bars that served organic wheatgrass was the pits. She might be left-wing in her politics, thought Fee, but she was a rampant snob in private.

Which was one reason that Fee had never told her parents about Dean. If she admitted to having a boyfriend her mother would have insisted on meeting him and then her parents would have judged him by appearances. Just like they did with everyone else – her included.

'Tattoos!' she could imagine her father saying. 'How utterly ghastly!'

'You live *where?* The Belgate estate? Oh dear!' Her mother wouldn't even try to hide her distaste.

Of course, Fee wasn't sure exactly where in Belgate Dean lived. All she knew was that he was staying with a mate while he saved up the cash to go travelling. When she'd asked for his address, Dean had made it clear that he hated what he called 'being hounded'.

'I'm a free spirit, Fee – I go where the wind blows!' he'd told her a couple of weeks before when she'd been pressing him to say when they could meet up again. 'And if you can't hack that, you'd better split now.'

The thought of losing him was more than she could contemplate. From that instant she had adopted the laid back, see-if-I-care approach – and it had worked. Until Sunday.

That was when she had admitted to him that she was only sixteen. And from that moment on, his calls had stopped.

What if he'd found someone else? Men did that all the time – even when they didn't have good reason. She should know. She only had to look at her own father.

Dad was still doing it. And this time, everyone would know about it. She could invent all the lies in the world but they wouldn't wash. Not any more.

She'd tried to cover up for him, she really had. It had only taken her a couple of seconds after Tanya had thrust that newspaper into her hand, for her to come back with a quick answer to explain away the irate expression on her father's face.

'Publicity stunt!' She had even managed a tight little laugh. 'Ratings always go up after something like that, and next month's storyline . . .'

'Come off it, Fee!' Tanya had mocked. 'We're not daft! Read that bit!'

She had stabbed at the newspaper and waited expectantly.

Fee had scanned the article.

Richard Bayliss, who plays the womanising Bradley French in **Fiddler's Wharf***, clearly takes the need to research his role very seriously. He was spotted last night in the exclusive Kiki's Club on the Fulham Road with teenage actress Sasha Sandrino. 'He was clearly not there for her conversation,' quipped a fellow club goer. 'They were all over one another!'*

She had felt sick. He couldn't start again.

'And look!' Tanya had snatched the paper from her hands and folded it in half. 'It says here, *On leaving the club, Bayliss spotted our photographer, lurched across the pavement and seconds after the above picture was taken, wrenched the camera from his hands and hurled it into the road.*'

'Dad hates being photographed,' Fee said dully, knowing even as she said it that it was a complete lie. Normally, her father was a real poser, welcoming any chance for publicity and spilling over with charm and largesse if he thought anyone was looking. Judging from the expressions on her friends' faces, they weren't fooled.

'It has to have been a set-up,' she had muttered. She had known that she was just digging the hole deeper but she had no choice.

'What goes on in our private lives is our business,' her mother always said. 'In public, it's a case of bright smile and sparkly eyes.'

A case of being plastic and pretentious, more like, Fee had thought, trying to avoid the enquiring glances of her friends.

'Anyway, got to dash!' she had mumbled, attempting a bright smile and shoving the paper back in Tanya's hand. 'Mum will—'

'Yes, of course!' Scarlett had cut in. 'She'll be dead cut up, won't she?'

'Do you think they'll get divorced?' Tanya had looked almost hopeful. 'You know, what with him flirting with that girl and—'

'Oh, for God's sake!' Fee had exploded, as her friend voiced her own silent fears. 'Do you believe everything you read in the newspapers? Are you that dumb?'

'Well, it's not an apparition in the photograph, is it?' Tanya had retorted. 'Or are you saying that the camera does lie after all?'

Fee had heard the sneer in her voice.

'Tanya, leave it!' Scarlett had snapped, as Fee stared at the newspaper again. She hadn't noticed the girl before, a tall, willowy figure standing behind her father, hands outstretched as if to restrain him, and a wide-eyed expression of shock on her face. The same look as Astrid had that night when Fee walked in . . .

'*Ze child — ze child is 'ere!*'

'*Get out, Fiona! Now!*'

The memory had triggered all the old feelings. Standing there beside her friends, Fee had felt physically sick. She didn't know what to say. Whatever she did say would be lies anyway. The evidence of the truth was in front of her.

'Fee, don't worry!' Scarlett had said, touching her arm. 'It's probably just a mix up — I'm sure your dad wouldn't do a thing like that . . .'

Oh, yes, he bloody would! Fee had wanted to scream. My dad does whatever he wants, when he wants and with whom he wants.

'*This is our little secret, Fee . . .*'

Scarlett had caught her arm as Fee had swayed towards her.

'Fee, are you OK?'

She had been saved from having to say anything by the unmistakable sound of her mobile phone shrilling from her jacket pocket.

Dean! He was phoning at last! The thought had snapped her back to the present.

'Must fly,' she had shouted, breaking into a run to get away from her mates. 'Catch you tomorrow!'

She had belted up the street, grabbing the phone and flicking open the cover.

'*Mum.*' The word had glared starkly up at her from the illuminated screen. '*Answer?*'

She had punched the 'No' button, and flipped the cover closed, her heart sinking. She couldn't talk to her mother, not now, not yet.

She had meant to go home straight away but when she reached the park, within sight of the back of the tall, three-storey house that they'd moved to only eighteen months before, something had stopped her. Perhaps if she gave them time, they'd have sorted it out. Dad would have come home, explained that it was all something about nothing, and everything would be OK.

Like – dream on.

What she didn't get was the fisticuffs bit. The flirting – oh sure; that was her father all right. But he wasn't violent – in fact, when they had fights on the set of *Fiddler's Wharf*, he was hopeless at it, said it turned his stomach. And when her mother had a go at him, shouting and slamming doors, he'd just walk down to the basement and start playing the piano and pretend it wasn't happening.

'*You love me, don't you, Fee?*' He used to pull her onto his lap when she was little, in the days before he was famous, when he was 'resting' more than he was acting and Fee's mother was calling him a waste of space and one of life's losers.

'*You'll make Daddy happy again, won't you?*'

But, she thought, shifting her position as stray leaves drifted down off the tree and landed in her lap, she hadn't made him happy. She couldn't. The older she got, the less she wanted to be paraded as the dutiful daughter in her designer dresses; the more she detested their materialistic, publicity-seeking lifestyle; the more she had felt like a misfit in her own home. She was sick of the way her father went all dewy eyed and came running to her every time he and Mum had a row; tired of bolstering his ego and telling him how fantastic he was.

And tired of trying to avoid being left on her own with him and having to listen to his constant bouts of self-pity.

The last few weeks had been the worst with her mother yelling at her for coming home late night after night and her father saying that the tension in the house was affecting his acting and her mother saying that acting was a rather inflated word for what he did.

But she'd coped with it all because she'd had Dean. The evenings spent with him, sometimes in a crowded club and sometimes buzzing round the county on the back of his battered motorbike, were sheer heaven. He'd told her that Harpleton was the pits, that just as soon as he'd saved the air fare he'd be off round the world. He'd even hinted, that special night at the party, that he couldn't bear to think about moving on unless she went with him.

'You're special, Fee,' he'd told her a dozen times. 'You and me, we're on the same wavelength.'

Sure, they were, she thought, brushing a falling leaf from her hair — until she blew it.

'Hey, can you do that again?'

She spun round and gasped as a flash bulb went off two inches in front of her face.

'What the...?'

'Sorry!' The tall guy looked sheepish. 'I couldn't resist —

64

you looked kind of dreamy and then those leaves fell on your head and you tipped—'

'What are you on?' Fee snapped, running her fingers through her hair. She paused. 'Hey, don't I know you?'

'BishAnd,' he nodded, using the school's nickname. 'Lyall Porter. Sorry about the picture, but it's for Art – well, Sculpture actually...'

'I don't care if it's for the ten o'clock news!' she retorted. 'I don't appreciate people taking...'

She stopped. That must have been what Dad felt like last night in the street. It didn't mean he'd been doing anything wrong. He just didn't like people sneaking up on him.

The relief made her grin broadly.

'What's so funny?' Lyall snapped.

'Nothing,' she said, shaking her head. 'Did you say sculpture?'

Lyall nodded.

'It's a new course,' he said. 'I'm going to be one of the first to do it.'

'I remember now! You're the arty guy from 10K, the one who made that chicken wire cowboy that's in Reception?'

Lyall nodded and looked chuffed.

'Dead clever,' she went on. 'I'm useless at all that kind of stuff. But what's taking my picture got to do with—'

'It's ideas!' Lyall enthused. 'See, I take loads of pictures and then kind of compose them into some sort of theme.'

He frowned.

'At least, I think that's what Mrs Faber meant,' he muttered, half to himself.

Fee grinned.

'If you understand a word of what that woman rattles on about, you're more clued up than me!' she said. 'Promise me one thing, though?'

'What?'

'If I look a total nerd, you won't show anyone the picture!'

Lyall grinned.

'Done!' he said. 'You might get made into a clay model, though!'

'You'll need a lot of clay,' Fee remarked wryly, adopting her usual habit of saying what she knew everyone else was thinking.

'What?' Lyall looked vaguely at her. 'You're Fiona Bayliss, aren't you? Your dad's the actor guy, isn't he? The one in—'

'So what if he is?'

Lyall held his hands up in mock surrender.

'Nothing – I was just making conversation. Must be nice though – I mean, having...'

He stopped in mid-sentence and kicked out viciously at a pile of fallen leaves.

'Having what?'

'Nothing – hey look at that!' He pointed across the park where a group of men were tossing carousel horses off a lorry. A couple of little kids were clambering all over them.

Fee couldn't see what he was on about.

'That would make an ace shot – see you!'

As Fee watched him belt across the grass and through the trees towards the fairground, she thought how cool it would be to have nothing more important to worry about than model making. She clambered to her feet as the clock on the church tower chimed six. She couldn't put it off any longer.

As she turned away and headed home for the scene she knew was waiting for her she couldn't decide which was worse – Dean's silence or her father's disloyalty.

There was only one thing she did know, and the knowledge made her feel physically sick.

Whichever way you looked at it, both were entirely her own fault.

* * *

'Lyall, you're late! Is everything OK?'

'What do you care?' He didn't break his stride but took the stairs two at a time, the camera bag bumping on his hip as he did so.

'Lyall!'

He could hear Maddy's sharp intake of breath, noted the brief pause before she spoke again.

'Tea will be ready in ten minutes,' she went on brightly. 'I've made spaghetti Bolognese, your favourite.'

He wanted to say he wasn't hungry, wanted to give her something to really worry about – but he wasn't about to pass up on pasta. He merely grunted and slammed his bedroom door behind him.

Despite everything, he had had an ace time for the past hour and a half. The Thursday market had been packing up in the town square and he'd polished off half a reel of film, snapping stallholders humping crates and joshing one another, throwing bits of over ripe fruit about and straining to take down awnings against the freshening wind. He taken pictures of a guy sleeping in a shop doorway, his manky dog sprawled across him like a kid's soft toy. And then he'd ended up in the park and taken that neat shot of Fiona as well as some really wacky fairground shots using those weird mirrors that make you look long and thin or short and fat. Real arty stuff, he thought.

But the coolest bit had been when one of the fairground guys had asked him if he was from the local press.

''Cos if so, mate, you might want to get a shot of the new AwesomeAwful ride. A killer that one − talk about G force!'

He had taken a shot, not so much because he needed one, but because he was so chuffed to be thought a proper person, a press photographer.

He had just three shots left on the film; he wanted to shoot them off tonight and then he could get Mrs Faber to develop it for him in the morning. Maybe he'd take some of Maddy and Patrick at supper − then again, maybe not. Why the hell should he show any interest in them any more?

'Tea's ready!' Patrick's gravelly tones echoed up the stairs.

For a moment he stood indecisively, the camera in his hands. Should he show them? Tell them about the Sculpture course? They didn't deserve to know; if they didn't want him as part of their lives any more, what business was it of theirs what he did?

But it might make them proud of him – they might even reconsider if they thought their foster kid was going to do something really good and worthwhile for once. They might want to hang around and see how it all panned out.

As he slumped down at the supper table, he made a big thing of slinging the camera bag over the back of the chair.

'Had a good day?' Patrick ventured as Lyall began forking spaghetti into his mouth.

Lyall shrugged and carried on eating.

'They tell us you didn't turn up at school yesterday,' Patrick said in the sort of voice that suggested he was trying to be very calm. 'What happened?'

Lyall shrugged again.

'What's that you've got?' Maddy jerked her head in the direction of the camera bag. 'Looks like a camera.'

'That's because it is a camera,' Lyall retorted.

'And where did that come from?' He could have sworn there was a note of wariness in Patrick's voice.

'I didn't steal it, if that's what you're thinking!' he snapped. 'I didn't skive off school to pinch stuff!'

Damn. Now he'd virtually admitted to skiving.

'Lyall, of course Patrick didn't...' Maddy began, pushing her plate away and resting her head on her arm.

'I don't steal any more,' he went on. 'You know that. Not like I used to.'

'We know, Lyall, and we're very proud of you,' Patrick concurred. 'Very proud indeed. We're just concerned about—'

'So why are you planning on dumping me then?'

Damn again. He hadn't meant to play it like that. Still, perhaps it was the best way after all – at least they wouldn't have time to make up dumb excuses or tell him half truths.

'How did...?' Maddy gasped. Her face, which was always pale, seemed almost transparent and Lyall noticed that there were dark shadows under her eyes. 'Who...?'

'It's not like that!' Patrick asserted almost simultaneously.

'So you're not going off somewhere then? You've changed your mind about not being able to cope with me?'

Now he'd started he couldn't stop. The ball of anger was getting bigger and the daggers were beginning to dig him in the middle of his brain.

'You don't understand...'

'Too damn right I don't understand!' He pushed back his chair and jumped to his feet, shoving the plate of half-eaten spaghetti across the table with such force that the salt and pepper pots went flying into Patrick's lap. 'I heard you the other night – whispering about not taking me with you and not coping.'

He could feel the heat racing up his neck, sense the sweat breaking out in his armpits.

'Well? Are you going somewhere? Yes or no?'

Patrick and Maddy looked at one another. Their silence told him all he needed to know.

'And am I coming?' There was just a chance he'd got it wrong. Or that they'd talked some more and decided they couldn't bear to part with him.

'Lyall, it's not that easy. Just listen for a minute...'

The pain in his brain was really bad now.

'You're fed up with me, right? Well, that's OK by me. 'Cos I was getting pretty damn tired of you too!'

'Lyall, I didn't mean for you to find out this way...' Maddy sounded close to tears.

'Oh, so how did you plan it then? Going to do a runner in the night, were you? Or were you going to get Jeff to tell me?'

He was used to them roping his social worker in when things got tricky.

'Of course not!' Patrick said. 'That is...I mean, we'd planned to tell you everything tonight, hadn't we, Maddy?'

His foster mother nodded.

'Just listen for a minute, Lyall, and we'll tell you...'

No!' He shoved his chair and the camera bag fell to the floor. 'You listen to me! I was thirteen, yeah? I'd been to three other foster homes. And you said I'd have a home with you for as long as I wanted. No matter what – that's what you said!'

He could have gone on, but he could feel his throat closing and the familiar pricking at the back of his eyes and no way on God's earth was he going to let them see him getting upset.

'And we meant it!' Maddy insisted. 'And it'll break our hearts but . . .'

She hesitated, chewing her lip and looking anxiously towards Patrick.

'Things happen, Lyall; things no one can plan for.'

'We're going to have to move house, Lyall. To Scotland,' Patrick said evenly, although Lyall could see his fingers working in his lap.

'Why?' Damn again. He hadn't meant to show an interest – or even to listen to their feeble excuses.

'Because – well, the thing is, you know that Maddy hasn't been . . .'

'Patrick's got a great new job!' Maddy interrupted brightly. 'Big promotion for him.'

'So why can't I come with you? I don't mind Scotland. Scotland's cool.'

Patrick shook his head.

'It's not as easy as that,' he began. 'There are other reasons.'

'Like what?'

'Well,' interrupted Maddy. 'Your social worker's here in Harpleton, and your counsellor—'

'So? I get new ones in Scotland. They're always leaving anyway, so what's the problem?'

'Lyall, you can't come to Scotland!' Patrick leapt to his feet. 'It's not up to you – the decision is made.'

'Patrick, for God's sake . . .' Maddy jumped up and then grabbed at the corner of the table for support.

'Maddy, are you OK?' Patrick was at her side in an instant.

'I'm fine, I'm fine!' She brushed him away. 'Listen, Lyall love—'

'Don't call me love!' he exploded. 'You don't love me. And I sure as hell HATE you!'

He snatched up the camera bag and pushed open the kitchen door.

'Lyall, come back!' Maddy was in tears and making no attempt to hide the fact. He knew he mustn't turn round because if he saw her cry, he'd start remembering the other stuff.

'Lyall, where did you get that camera?' This was Patrick, bearing down on him with a worried look on his face.

'You want to know? I'll tell you!' Despite his resolve, Lyall spun round. 'Mrs Faber lent it to me because I'm going to do GCSE Sculpture. She says I'm very good! Surprised, are you? Surprised anyone thinks I'm worth anything?'

In one stride Maddy was at his side, her arm thrown round his shoulder.

'Lyall, we think you're terrific!' she pleaded. 'We love you and we won't go till we know you've got somewhere nice to go and—'

Lyall shoved her away and she reeled back, hitting her hip on the corner of the Welsh dresser.

'That's enough!' Patrick shouted. 'Just get upstairs, Lyall, and calm down. We'll talk about this – and your truancy – tomorrow when Jeff's here!'

So they had roped Jeff in after all! In fact – and the thought hit him like a blow between the eyes as he bolted along the hall and out of the front door, ignoring Maddy's cries of alarm – Jeff had known all about this long before Lyall had an inkling. Jeff was in on it.

They were all ganging up against him.

Well, sod the lot of them.

Stuff them, stuff them, stuff them. He pounded down the pavement, his feet keeping rhythm with his muttered shouts.

He'd show them. He didn't need them.

It was a good thing they were going.

He'd had it up to here with so-called carers.

He'd do just fine on his own.

And this time, he wouldn't mess up.

This time he wouldn't kill anyone.

Except, perhaps, just perhaps, himself.

4

'Here she is! Just hang on – I'll be right back.'

Fee's heart sank as she heard her mother's over-bright tones echoing from the sitting room and realised she wasn't alone. She didn't want to make polite conversation with one of her ghastly friends. Someone who'd seen the headline, no doubt, and dashed round to gloat. She felt sick and was beginning to wish she hadn't eaten so much chocolate.

'For God's sake, where have you been?' Fee's mother closed the door and hissed at Fee under her breath. 'All hell's been let loose here – your father—'

'I know, I saw the paper,' Fee interrupted, shrugging her school bag off her shoulder and dumping it on the stairs. 'Where's Dad?'

Her mother's lips tightened into a thin line.

'Heading up the M1 as we speak, if he knows what's good for him!' she muttered, grabbing Fee by the elbow and propelling her into the kitchen. 'Now listen, we're playing this right down, you understand me? We trust your father totally, any suggestions about bad behaviour are too ludicrous to comment on – that sort of thing.'

She held Fee's gaze.

'You understand me? The main thing we have to do is show solidarity, squash the rumours. OK?'

Fee was prevented from replying by the shrilling of the

phone on the wall. Instinctively she stretched out a hand to answer it.

'Leave it!' Her mother spat out the words. 'It's been like that ever since lunch time – the press wanting a quote! Which is why Max is here.'

'Max?'

'Max Crombie,' explained her mother. 'The one who did that lovely piece about us all for *Hello!* magazine last spring. You must remember!'

Fee remembered all right. It had been bad enough having to endure two whole days of stupid posing – standing by her father, and gazing up adoringly at him; holding her sister's hand (that was vomit inducing in itself because Louise kept giggling like a twelve-year-old on speed), or perching on the patio wall in the sort of clothes she would normally rather die than touch. But the worst part had been when the magazine hit the newsstands and all her mates at school saw the sugary sludge that passed for journalistic prose. It was weeks before they had stopped teasing her about 'Fiona's pastel painted bedroom inspired by her childhood home in Devon' and 'Fiona prepares for a night out with big sister Louise.' As if.

'. . . and he's such a poppet, dear Max!' her mother was enthusing.

'Oh sure!' retorted Fee cynically. 'Such a poppet that he couldn't wait to speed up here and dish the dirt on Dad!'

'Keep your voice down and use your brain!' her mother hissed. 'I asked him to come. He was the first person I phoned when the *Chronicle* ran that wretched picture in the lunch time issue. You won't believe it – Anton was halfway through doing my highlights, head full of foil strips, the lot—'

'You asked him?' Fee couldn't believe her ears. 'So what's all this drivel about squashing rumours?'

'The best way to shut people up is to let them think there's no story!' her mother replied. 'I'm not in the business of image making for nothing – and God knows I've had enough practice on your father.'

She patted her already immaculate hair into place and gave Fee a gentle shove towards the door.

'Now we go in there with bright smiles and...'

'...sparkly eyes!' finished Fiona. 'I know – I've been here before, remember?'

Satisfied that for once, even if momentarily, her mother was lost for words, she marched into the sitting room.

'Pretty dead embarrassing for you, all this?' Max had stood up and was holding out his hand to Fiona. She ignored it and went to the far end of the room and perched on the window seat. She really did feel sick; that last Aero bar had been a big mistake.

Max wasn't put off.

'How do you feel about all your mates reading this stuff in the paper? I mean, the girl he was with was only a bit older than you and—'

For a brief nanosecond, Fee toyed with the idea of telling him exactly what she was thinking, but she could feel her mother's eyes drilling into her side.

She fixed a bright smile on her face.

'Frankly,' she said, 'it doesn't bother me. My real friends know it's a load of rubbish, and those that think differently aren't worth worrying about.'

She could hear the relief in her mother's instant exhalation of breath.

Max inclined his head ever so slightly to one side and suppressed a grin.

'So, Helen,' he went on smoothly, turning to Fee's mother, 'you want me to get in quick with a piece to stress – what exactly? I mean, rumour has it that this isn't the first time Richard has—'

'Let me put it this way, Max,' her mother interrupted, crossing her legs and showing just enough thigh for Max to momentarily lose his place in his notebook. 'Richard's one of our top actors . . .'

That's rich, thought Fee. How did it usually go?

That show is so predictable, Richard . . . call yourself an actor . . . if you had any sort of ambition you'd be at Stratford on Avon, not in some far-fetched soap opera . . .

' . . . bound to resent the constant media attention, especially when he was with poor little Sasha Sandrino.'

Fee did a double take at the same moment as Max raised an enquiring eyebrow.

'So you knew about his relationship with . . .'

'Hardly a relationship, Max darling!' she laughed. 'Look, this is absolutely confidential and truly, you mustn't write it in the piece – the TV company would kill me – but – well, Sasha is an ambitious little thing and she's auditioning to play the part of . . .'

She broke off to cough delicately behind her hand and clear her throat. Max passed the water jug that was sitting on the coffee table, but Fee wasn't taken in. That was her mother's tried and tested response before telling a barefaced lie. She didn't realise her daughter had sussed it, but then again, there was an awful lot about Fee that her mother didn't know.

'Thank you.' She sipped delicately and dabbed her mouth with her forefinger.

'Well, let's just say that Sasha wants the part of Bradley French's long lost daughter in *Fiddler's Wharf* and frankly Rich isn't at all sure she is capable of cutting the mustard.'

Max cocked his head to one side and scribbled furiously.

'He's taken her under his wing – he can't bear to see these poor young actresses mess up on their first big chance. Much better to persuade her not to go for the role, than have her fail and ruin her chances of other parts. But the press . . .'

Here we go, thought Fee. Cue moist eyes.

'They see a man of Richard's standing out with a young girl and immediately think the worst. Why, Max, why?'

'Bad news sells papers,' Max replied. 'And you must admit, he did grab that cameraman's gear and throw it to the ground. Hardly the action of a man with nothing to hide.'

'Oh Max, Max!' Her mother leaned towards him, and Fee cringed at the amount of cleavage being thrust under Max's aquiline nose. 'Look at that photo again.'

She pushed the paper towards him.

'What do you see?'

Max peered at the picture and shrugged.

'Your husband looking as if he'd like to throttle the photographer, Sasha about to burst into tears . . .'

'What you see,' Fee's mother asserted, 'is Richard glaring at the photographer who was too busy taking his picture to get out of the way and let Richard take Sasha to her car. Of course she's close to tears, bless her – to be told she had no hope of the part . . .'

For a long moment there was silence in the room. Then Max threw back his head and roared with laughter.

'I can see why the Labour Party want you on board, Helen!' he chuckled. 'When it comes to image manipulation—'

'Management, Max, please. Management!'

Fee's mother had the expression of one who has been mortally wounded.

Max stood up.

'I'll see what I can do – but if that photographer presses charges . . .'

He let the sentence hang unfinished in the air.

'He won't,' Fee's mother assured him, opening the sitting-room door and leading him into the hall. 'Trust me. He won't.'

At that moment, a key turned in the front door.

'Hello, people! I'm back!'

It was her father. And he was clearly using all his acting skills to the full.

'How are my girls?' He flung open his arms and Fee's mother went all girly-girly and hugged him as if he'd just returned from eight months in the Antarctic.

Part of Fee wanted to hang around and hear what he had to say for himself. Or rather, what her mother had programmed him to say. But she couldn't.

'Hi, Bambi!' Her father grinned at her, but she dodged his open arms and ran up the stairs.

'Fiona!' Under normal circumstances, the sharpness of her mother's tone would have brought her to an abrupt halt. But these weren't normal circumstances. She didn't dare open her mouth to reply.

She only just made it into the bathroom in time.

Vaguely she heard her parents calling her name, but there was still no way she could respond.

She was far too busy throwing up.

★ ★ ★

The churchyard seemed to have come to life in the dusky light of the early September evening. In one corner, on a rickety iron seat, a couple were snogging and close to the crumbling stone wall behind the church, an elderly man was arranging fresh flowers in a jam-jar beside a marble edged grave.

Lyall hadn't a clue why he'd come here. He'd just known he had to get the hell out of the house before he exploded. He wasn't going to hang around feeling like a spare part. He had run flat out for ages, and would have gone on running, if he hadn't bumped into that guy Jason from school – the one they all called Midget – grappling with a dent in his bike. He'd offered to help but the guy was all up himself and had hardly spoken a word to him. That had got him furious again, so he'd just run and run until the stitch in his side forced him to stop, and this was where he'd found himself, slumped down by that Frederick person's grave, panting in an attempt to catch his breath.

He felt as if, any moment, his head might burst open. How could they do this? Make plans and not tell him? Not even listen to what he had to say? What was it they used to say to him – 'We're your family, Lyall – we're all in this together!' Like hell they were.

He grabbed an empty beer can lying in the unmown grass by the grave and hurled it across the path; watched it arc in the air and drop to earth. And disappear.

That's when he saw it – the gaping rectangle, freshly dug, the moist earth piled neatly beside it.

A shiver fluttered through his spine. Somewhere, someone was lying dead, ready to be dropped into that hole, covered up and left to rot.

If he died, would they put him in a grave? He staggered to his feet and edged closer to the hole, imagining the coffin slowly being lowered, hearing the quiet sobbing of Maddy and Patrick. Would they erect a tombstone with fancy writing and a fat cherub on the top; or would they burn his body and forget that he'd ever existed? He'd want a grave; he'd want Maddy and Patrick to sit there and suffer, wishing they'd been nicer to him, wishing they hadn't been the cause of his death.

The memories came trickling back.

'It's not your fault, Lyall — no one is blaming you . . .'

The woman with the red hair had squatted down and peered into his eyes.

'She was sick, Lyall — you weren't to know. . .'

But he had known. That's why he'd given her the pink medicine, the one his mum always gave them when they cried and she needed them to shut up and give her a few moments' peace. He could see himself now, fighting to get the sticky top off the bottle, crying with frustration because his little fingers couldn't grip tightly enough to undo it. And then finally managing and pouring the stuff into a spoon and shouting at Candy because she wouldn't open her mouth wide enough and . . .

'Candy!'

His fist slammed into the side of his head as he shouted her name. He mustn't think about her. He turned from the newly dug grave but the images wouldn't go. She was hovering there, in front of his eyes, her little face flushed scarlet, her wide eyes not leaving his.

'Me hurting, Lyall.'

When she'd spewed up the medicine all over his T-shirt and just stared at him, unblinking and uncaring, he'd realised he had to be naughty, had to do what he knew would end in another beating.

'If you leave this flat while I'm out, I'll bloody kill you!'

But his mum had been gone for three bedtimes. It was

usually only one; but this time the biscuits and crisps she'd left had all gone, and the bit of milk in the bottom of the carton was smelling funny. And Candy was getting sicker.

Lyall kicked out at a tree stump. He had to stop remembering. Remembering was for idiots. He grabbed the camera from the bag on his shoulder, slipped the strap over his head and began focusing his mind on framing a picture.

Think about the picture, think about the course, don't think about . . .

'You look after your sister, you hear me? You're a big boy now.'

The door had been locked, of course; she always locked them in for their own good. But she was right; he was a big boy. He was seven and he wasn't stupid. He knew where the spare door key was kept. He'd climbed onto the stool, onto the table and then, standing on tiptoe and stretching as high as he could, he'd managed to get the key off the top of the door frame.

Then he'd tied Candy to the table leg, just like his mum used to do with him. And he'd run.

Only he hadn't been fast enough.

He hadn't made people understand quickly enough.

He'd messed up.

Take the picture, stop thinking. He looked through the viewfinder but his hands were shaking and the images were wobbling and distorted.

'Oh my God! What have you done?'

Then the sirens.

And the men in green.

'Get the lad out of here!'

And he'd kicked them and punched them and tried to grab hold of Candy but they were all too big for him and he was lifted higher and higher into someone's arms and they'd taken him away.

They hadn't even let him have Kangaroo. They said Kangaroo was dirty and smelly and they'd get him a new one.

But he hadn't wanted a new one. He'd wanted the one he'd got, with its threadbare tail and the pouch that you could hide Smarties in for later.

But they hadn't listened. No one ever did.

'That's an interesting choice of subject, I must say!' Lyall wheeled round, his hands still gripping the camera.

A woman in a pair of faded jeans and a polo shirt was grinning at him and gesturing towards the freshly-dug grave.

Lyall stuffed the camera into its bag.

'Hey, don't let me stop you!' she went on. 'Photography your hobby, is it?'

Lyall shrugged. He wasn't about to start making small talk with strangers.

'Don't I recognise you?' the woman went on. 'I know – you were here earlier. You had a run-in with my verger.'

Oh God. It was the vicar woman.

'You haven't got that white collar thing – I didn't realise...'

Hang on. What was he doing, making polite conversation? Just get the hell out of here.

She laughed.

'It's not glued to my neck, you know,' she remarked. 'Sometimes I like to discard the thing and just be Sue – not Vicar, or Reverend or whatever else people like to call me. So why are you photographing a new grave? Oh, golly, you're not a relative, are you? Of the deceased, I mean?'

'She's gone, Lyall. She's not coming back. You must try to forget...'

'I'm so sorry!' The vicar touched his arm and peered anxiously into his face. He realised his eyes were damp. 'How stupid of me! Only no one said...'

'That's nothing to do with me! I was just...practising.' It wasn't strictly true but it would shut her up.

'Really? Is this school stuff or what? Sorry – I don't know your name?'

Lyall said nothing. It didn't do to get familiar with religious types.

She didn't seem fazed.

'I mean, you can take pictures inside the church if it would help – there are some lovely old carvings and—'

'It's for GCSE Sculpture!' He was astonished to hear himself speak. 'I've got to take a load of pictures and then decide which ones to use as models for my sculpture.'

'How terrific!' she gasped. 'I've always wished I was arty but me – I can't even arrange a vase of flowers!'

She grinned and pulled a face.

'Well, feel free to use the church when you want to. It's locked most of the time, I'm afraid, but I can let you in.'

'What?' Only a few hours before, they'd been trying to

get him away from the place. Well, not her, but the other guy.

'The vicarage is Number 7,' she continued. 'That red brick monstrosity across the street! You never know, you might get some inspiration.'

She looked at her watch.

'Oh heavens! Must dash – I'm supposed to be at a PCC meeting and I'm already late. See you around, I hope.'

'What happens when you're dead?'

The words came from nowhere and his mouth dropped open as he realised he'd uttered them.

The vicar stopped in her tracks and turned round, her face serious now, a slight frown creasing her brow.

'That's a big question – one I haven't got time to do justice to right now but—'

'So you don't know, right?' He spat the words out.

Typical. They pretended to be so clever but in the end, they were just the same as you. No answers to anything that really mattered.

'No one knows – but I can tell you what I believe. I believe that when people die, they go to a place where they are loved and cherished and cared for like never before and all the pain they ever had fades away and—'

'Go to hell!' Now the anger was taking over and it had come from nowhere. No slow simmering, no warning, just a searing explosion of hot fury that was threatening to swallow him up.

He caught the look of astonishment on the woman's

face, saw her take a step towards him, and knew he had to beat it and fast.

As he pounded along the path and out into the street, he heard her voice calling after him.

'We'll talk about it another day, OK?'

Talk about what? he thought. About how I didn't care for Candy enough and now someone else is, and she knows I mucked up? Or talk about how, if I die, someone somewhere will love me lots – and never change?

Talking sucks anyway. You can never trust what people say.

It's what they do that counts.

And that sucks too.

* * *

'£10 and that's your lot, get it?'

'We're quits now, so don't try any clever stuff with me, OK?'

Jay lay on his bed staring up at the ceiling and rehearsing what he was going to say to Rick the following morning. Of course, he hadn't actually got the money yet; he would have to ask Nan for it at breakfast time. And anyway, who was he kidding? He knew deep down that he'd never say any of those clever things to Rick; he'd just shove the money at him and pray that he'd leave him alone.

Not for the first time, he wished he wasn't such a wimp. Take this evening – just thinking about it made him cringe. He'd been so wet, not once but twice. And he hated himself for it.

He'd never delivered the evening papers so fast in all his life. He had pedalled furiously up and down the alleys and walkways of the estate in the steady drizzle, almost ripping the *Chronicle* as he stuffed it through each letter box. Sometimes the brightly coloured leaflets about the Town Fair which had been slipped into each copy, would fall into a puddle and he'd just leave them there, so desperate was he to get back home.

And then, taking the corner of Windermere Way and Ullswater Court a bit too fast, he had skidded on his bike and careered straight into a twin buggy being pushed by a middle-aged woman with a German Shepherd on a lead. The impact threw him from the saddle, over the handlebars and into the gutter. Papers spilled onto the damp roadway.

'What the ****!' The woman had screeched at him, as one of the toddlers in the buggy began to yell. 'You could have flaming killed them!'

'I'm so sorry,' he had begun, faltering as nausea hit him and a knife-like pain seared through his shoulder. The dog was barking, straining on its leash and was so uncomfortably close that Jay scrambled to his feet and staggered backwards. As he bent to retrieve the scattered newspapers, the ground beneath him seemed to spin and lurch.

'I'll give you bloody sorry, you hooligan!' the woman had shouted. 'You tell him, Tiger!'

She jerked the dog's lead and it barked even more furiously.

'It was an accident, honestly!' Jay had ventured again, stuffing damp papers into the sack and desperately trying to ignore his stinging elbows and knees. He had wanted to grab the bike and get the hell out of it, but the dog was standing between him and the cycle and no way was he going to go one centimetre nearer. 'The kids are all right though, aren't they?'

The woman had glanced at the two children, pulled a dummy from her pocket and stuffed it into the mouth of the one that was yelling.

'No thanks to you!' she had retorted. 'You teenagers – you've no sense of responsibility. You have life too bloomin' easy, if you ask me!'

With that she yanked the buggy off the kerb, shouted, 'Heel!' at the dog, and stomped off up the road without a backward glance.

And that's when it happened. It was as if someone – or something – else had got inside his head. He had stood there, the woman's words echoing in his ears.

'You have life too bloomin' easy...'

'Oh sure yes!**** easy!' His nan had taught him never, ever to swear but now it was as if some hidden floodgate had opened. 'You try living with a mad woman, you try getting picked on every day at school, you try not having a mum or...'

That was when the tears had come. He'd tried to stop, of course he had; guys of sixteen don't blub and certainly not in the street. But he couldn't. He'd grabbed his bike, seen the twisted mudguard, realised he couldn't ride the thing till he'd sorted it, and just cried some more, looking over his shoulder to check no one could see. His shoulder had been hurting like hell, his scratches stung like crazy – but the worst pain had been inside his head.

For just a moment, he could remember her. A pink and white diamond-patterned skirt this time, a smell like wood smoke, and hair that he could wind round his tiny fingers and cuddle while he sucked his thumb.

The sound of her voice – 'Mama kiss it better, Jay-Jay, all better now...'

And then it was gone.

'You should have been here! Nan should be your problem, not mine!'

He knew, even as he shouted the words into the air, that it wasn't her fault she'd died. Nan had told him that often enough.

'It was your dad's fault – good for nothing waster that he was!' she would say. 'But then, least said soonest mended.'

And that was it. All he knew was that Barbara, his mum, had been driving a car because his father was dead drunk, a lorry had come round the corner on the wrong side of the road and she'd been killed instantly. His father had died a week later in hospital.

'Why, why, why?' He had pounded the saddle of his bike with his fists, not that he'd really known what it was he was questioning – whether it was the reason for her death, or for his nan's dottiness or even his own tears.

'You OK, mate?'

Jay had heard the question before he saw the big guy panting to a halt beside him.

'Yeah, fine thanks!' He had kept his eyes averted as he picked up the bike and turned it for home.

'Want some help straightening it out?' the guy asked, dropping down onto one knee and hitching a bag over his shoulder. 'Looks pretty simple.'

He gripped the mudguard with both hands.

'If you just take hold of the . . .'

Jay realised with a jolt that it was Lyall Porter from school. Jay hardly knew him; he was in a different tutor group from Jay, but he'd seen him sitting outside the head's study often enough to guess he must be a troublemaker and frankly, Jay had had enough of thugs to last him a lifetime.

'No, I'm cool!' With that, he had yanked the bike out of Lyall's grasp, and broken into a run, pushing the bike and praying that he wouldn't be followed.

Lying on the bed now, rubbing his bruised shoulder, he knew that he should have delivered the remaining few papers instead of dashing home, but at the time, he simply couldn't be bothered. It was as if all the energy had drained from his body, leaving him feeling limp and empty. He'd probably be for it from the Patels in the morning; but hopefully no one would make a complaint.

Perhaps if he hadn't felt so wrung out, he'd have coped better with what happened later. It was after he had cooked supper, washed up and hung out the washing that

Nan had left in the machine all day, that his grandmother had announced that she was going out.

'Out where?' Alarm bells had started ringing in his head even before his nan had slipped her arms into her raincoat.

'Only round to Beryl's,' she had replied. 'She's got the new catalogue in and . . .'

Relief had washed over him. Beryl had moved in three doors down a couple of months back, and she and Nan really hit it off – were almost best friends already. What's more, she was as sane and normal as he was and he knew that if Nan did or said anything odd round there, Beryl would know what to do.

'Have a great time, then!' he had smiled. 'Don't rush back.'

He had been halfway through his English assignment when the doorbell had rung.

'Oh Nan!' he'd muttered under his breath as he had pounded down the stairs. 'Forgotten your key again, I suppose!'

But it wasn't his nan.

It was Rick and Matt.

'We'd like that tenner now,' Rick had drawled, pulling on the gum lodged between his teeth.

'How did you know. . . ?' Jay had begun

' . . . where you live?' Matt had given a short, spiteful laugh. 'We can find out anything we need to know, right, Rick?'

Rick had nodded slowly.

'So just get the dosh, mate, OK?'

'I haven't got it right now,' Jay had told them, hating himself for the quaver in his voice. 'I was going to get it from the cash machine on the way to school.'

'Oh very swanky!' Rick had retorted. 'But it won't do, I'm afraid. We want it now.'

Jay swallowed hard.

'You'll have to wait,' he said, trying to shut the door in their faces. But Rick was quicker than he was and within a second, both he and Matt were in the hallway, eyeing Jay up and down.

'So where does your gran keep her cash then?' Rick demanded, pushing Jay out of the way and striding through to the kitchen. 'In here – or here?'

He began pulling drawers open while Matt hovered in the doorway, looking a trifle uneasy.

'There isn't any money!' Jay shouted. 'Honestly! I'll give it to you in the morning.'

'So!' Rick strode through to the living room and cast his eye round the small, cluttered room. 'Aha!'

Within an instant, he had flung open the door of the sideboard and grabbed a bottle of whisky and a couple of miniature brandies.

'These'll do for starters!' he announced triumphantly, waving the Johnnie Walker above his head. 'But if we don't get the cash tomorrow—'

'You will – you can't take those, my gran—'

But he knew there was no point. Rick was already at the door, kicking it open and unscrewing the cap from the whisky.

'Ten quid, remember!' he taunted. 'First thing!'

With that, he quaffed some scotch from the bottle and swaggered off down the street, with Matt in hot pursuit.

After that, Jay couldn't concentrate. He tried to apply his mind to his assignment but it was too full of other things. That fleeting memory he'd had of his mum, his worries about Nan, the fact that by tomorrow he not only had to have the cash for Rick but a good excuse to tell Miss Perry and Mr Sinclair why he wouldn't be going on the French exchange.

Now, lying on his bed, he let himself imagine what it might be like if he really could go. It would be dead cool to spend two whole weeks in Poitiers. He could just imagine himself, drinking wine and eating all those squidgy French cheeses, riding a bike through the countryside and never having to watch the time because Nan might be in a state. Perhaps he could go; perhaps he could persuade Beryl to keep an eye on Nan. Dumb idea! It wasn't a freebie, it was an exchange; you had to have the French guy back at your place and no way could he have anyone to stay here. There was no spare bedroom and besides, what if Nan dished up some foul food like the sandwich? It was a non-starter and there was no point wishing.

'I'm back!' His nan's voice jolted him from his daydream, and he leapt off the bed as the front door slammed and ran to the top of the stairs.

'Well, I must say, I've had a lovely time!' his grandmother exclaimed, hanging her coat up and smiling up at him. 'We had a nice long chat and I ordered stuff from the catalogue – a nice dressing gown for you and some slippers, and a skirt for me.'

Jay dreaded to think what his nan's idea of nice was, but at least she seemed happy and normal.

'So have you done your homework?' she asked. 'It's time you were in bed, you know.'

He didn't bother telling her that sixteen-year-olds didn't go to bed at nine fifteen. He just nodded – and then he remembered.

'Nan, can you lend me ten pounds?' he asked. 'I'll pay you back tomorrow – I'll go to the bank on the way home and—'

'Ten pounds? What can you possibly want ten pounds for?'

'School stuff,' he said vaguely. 'Please, Nan . . .'

'All right!' She opened her bag and threw her purse up the stairs. 'Take what you want – I'm just going to make a cuppa.'

He opened the purse. All that was inside it was a ten pence piece and her bus pass.

'Nan!' He thundered down the stairs and into the kitchen. 'There's no money in here. Look!'

She snatched the purse from him and stared at it.

'My money! Where is it? It's gone!'

She looked at him in a panic.

'Who's taken it? Did you take it? Did you?'

She was shouting now and wagging her finger at him.

'No, Nan, of course I didn't—'

'You thought you could get away with it again, didn't you? Thought I was stupid. Well, let me tell you—'

'NAN, shut up!' he shouted. 'I haven't got your money. I wish to God I had, but I haven't. What have you done with it?'

She sat down heavily on the kitchen chair and began rocking backwards and forwards.

'They've stolen it,' she sobbed. 'Taken it away. It's him, of course – she'd never do a thing like that, not my Barbara, never, never . . .'

He'd had it. He couldn't hack this any more.

'Nan, stop it! Just think!' He grabbed her wrists and sank down on his knees in front of her. 'Think!'

She stared at him blankly.

'I bet you gave it to Beryl, yes?' he urged. 'You ordered stuff from the catalogue and gave Beryl—'

'Beryl!' She jumped to her feet. 'You say Beryl's got it? How dare she take my money! I always knew that woman wasn't all she was cracked up to be!'

When he looked back on that moment hours later, he couldn't believe what he'd done. He hadn't even been aware that he had grabbed her shoulders and was shaking her, not until she began to cry.

'Don't! You're hurting me!'

His arms fell to his side. He stared at her in horror.

'Nan, I'm sorry, really – I'm so sorry!' He was almost in tears himself. 'I didn't mean to . . . it's just that you don't understand and—'

'I understand one thing,' she retorted sternly, tossing her head. 'Bed for you, young man! You're over tired.'

Jay opened his mouth to speak and then closed it again. A huge wave of weariness washed over him, making his limbs feel as heavy as lead.

'Are you OK?' he asked softly. 'We'll find the money tomorrow, don't you worry.'

'Money?' she asked. 'What are you talking about? What money?'

Jay managed to get halfway upstairs before he started to cry.

5

She is standing on the landing in her Winnie the Pooh nightshirt, shivering and wondering what to do. Daddy's in a bad mood, has been all day long, because his play has flopped and the newspapers said nasty things about his acting. He shouted at her when she spilt her milk at tea time and said he didn't have time to read her a story or play a game before she went to bed. And she knows that when Daddy is in a mood he has to be left alone. Mummy says so.

But Mummy isn't here. Mummy and Louise have gone to Paris because Louise is going to be on the front of a magazine and make lots of money. Fiona can't go; Fiona's just a kid. She wishes they hadn't gone because her tummy hurts and her head is aching and she wants Mummy to give her the yellow fizzy tablet that makes pains go away.

Then she hears someone laughing. She creeps along the landing and pushes open the door of her parents' room. Mummy's back! She can see her head on the pillow, one arm thrown across Daddy. Daddy's cuddling Mummy and telling her she's pretty and lovely and special and all his.

'Mummy!'

She runs towards the bed and tries to climb in.

But it isn't Mummy.

It's Astrid, the au pair girl. And she hasn't got any clothes on. 'Ze child is 'ere – ze child is 'ere!'

Astrid is screaming. Daddy swings his legs out of bed. He hasn't got any clothes on either and he looks very very angry.

Fiona is angry too. This isn't like it's meant to be. Fiona is Daddy's special girl, and Mummy's special too — but Astrid is just 'the girl' — that's what Mummy calls her. Fiona doesn't want Astrid, she wants Mummy.

Now she's crying great gulping sobs.

'Get out of here, now!' Her father's coming nearer.

Fiona throws up all over the carpet.

Daddy smacks her.

Hard.

Fiona jolted up in bed, the scream dying on her lips as the shaft of light pouring through her bedroom curtains jerked her back to reality. She knew at once it was just a dream and yet the feeling of anger and shock was as real as it had been nine years ago.

And the words were still reverberating in her head.

'Get out of here, now!'

Only this time it was her mother's strident tones, interspersed with choked back sobs, that echoed down the landing. A door slammed. Fee held her breath.

A shaft of muted light streaked across her bedroom carpet as her own bedroom door slowly swung open. Through half-closed eyelids, she saw the silhouette of her father, breathing heavily, standing there, watching her.

She forced her breathing to be slow and measured, exaggerated the rise and fall of her chest under the duvet so that he would think she was sound asleep.

'Fee?' His whisper was hoarse in his throat as he took a couple of steps closer to the bed.

She ignored it. There had been times, so many times, when she hadn't turned a deaf ear, when she had sat up in bed and he had slumped down beside her and poured out his heart to her. He'd done it when she was too little to understand the words, but quite big enough to know that she was meant to take care of Daddy because he was sad. He'd done it when she thought that the fondling and the cuddling was just a sign that Daddy loved her to bits and wanted her to know everything about him.

But now she was grown up; now she knew that it wasn't really his heart he was sharing with her, just his own, twisted version of reality.

It had happened on what she still called The Astrid Night. He'd come into her room, said he was sorry about the smack and asked if she would forgive her nasty angry Daddy. And when, through her sniffs, she had nodded, he had pulled her onto his lap and made her promise faithfully never, ever to tell Mummy about what she'd seen. Because if she did, Daddy would go away and Fiona would never see him again. Mummy didn't love Daddy like she should do, he told her, which was why sometimes Daddy needed lots of cuddles and hugs to cheer him up. If Mummy didn't shout so much, Daddy would be happy; and of course, if Fiona told Mummy what she had seen, Mummy would shout even more than usual and that would be horrid, wouldn't it?

When Fee had nodded and smiled at Daddy, he'd told her that if she really was very good, and promised to forget all about what she'd seen, he would buy her that big new bicycle she wanted and she wouldn't have to wait until Christmas. Wouldn't that be nice?

She'd got her bicycle but she'd hardly ever ridden it because every time she sat on the saddle she remembered that night, and remembering was breaking her promise. Best not ride the bicycle.

Sitting up in bed now, her knees pulled up under her chin, Fee found herself shaking her head in disbelief at the child who was so gullible, so easily taken in. She'd really believed she had it in her power to keep Daddy happy by keeping his secrets. She'd felt so important, so proud.

So important, in fact, that when Daddy wanted more hugs and longer kisses from her, she gave those to him too. She was the peacekeeper and she relished the role.

Fee peered at the clock beside her bed. 4 a.m. She threw back the duvet, slipped her bathrobe over her shoulders and walked to the window. Through the trees, she could make out the looming shapes of roller coasters and the AwesomeAwful ride that all the newspapers were on about and the white expanse of the giant marquees. She tried to kill the bad dream by thinking about the Fair, but her brain was filled with images of Astrid.

It was odd; she could remember Astrid's features as if it were only yesterday that she'd found her in her mother's place on the window side of the king size bed. Pointed nose, huge eyes, full lips and long blonde hair; that was something all the other women – or at least, the ones she knew about – had in common; big noses and blonde hair. A ripple of dread shuddered through her body when she recalled that the girl in the newspaper picture the day before had them both too. Dad's tastes clearly hadn't changed.

Maybe, she thought, wiping the condensation off the window with the back of her hand and staring out into the darkness, that was why her mother had her hair coloured every five minutes. Fee had inherited her mother's dark brown locks and on more than one occasion, her mother had suggested she should have highlights, or low lights or even a brand new colour.

'No one wants to go through life looking nondescript, darling!' her mother would trill. 'And it never does any harm to give your genes a helping hand!'

Remembering her mother's oft-repeated phrase, Fee's hand strayed instinctively to her stomach.

What if she really was pregnant? What if, right now, inside her, a tiny little embryo was taking shape, dark hair and all? What if she was, without knowing it, a mother herself?

For a split second, she could see herself with a baby in her arms, a smiling, chubby little thing, clinging onto her finger for dear life. And for that moment, she felt a warm glow, something almost verging on excitement. Her own baby. A baby she would love and cherish and never, ever criticise or talk about behind its back. They'd be great parents, her and Dean . . .

The euphoria disappeared in a flash. She wasn't ready for this; not yet, not now. Not on her own. But she wouldn't be on her own, would she? Because if she was pregnant, it wouldn't be just hers. It would be Dean's too, and he'd be by her side, looking after her and standing up to her parents and...

The thought of her parents' reaction made her feel physically sick again. She had to find Dean. Fast. She had to tell him. But would he want to know? Only four days ago, he'd accused her of telling barefaced lies, of leading him on and trying to be something she wasn't. She'd shouted back, told him that it wasn't her fault, but he wouldn't listen. He'd stormed off; and she hadn't heard a word since.

But it was true – it hadn't been her fault, not really. If he hadn't asked her to the night club, she would never have needed to lie. She crawled back into bed and pulled the duvet up round her neck, remembering that first night at The Melting Pot. When the bus had pulled up at the corner of St James Street, she had very nearly decided to stay put and go home. The Melting Pot was Harpleton's newest, trendiest club and the pavement outside was crowded with stylish twenty-somethings queuing to get in, the girls all dressed in the kind of clothes that had guys ogling and made Fiona feel drab and boring despite her black leather trousers and new silver grey camisole.

But then she had spotted Dean pushing his way through the throng of people and edging nearer the canopied entrance. She had leapt off the bus in the nick of time and crossed the road, dodging the taxis that were pulling up in droves.

By the time she had reached the entrance, Dean had disappeared.

'ID?'

The burly-shouldered bouncer on the door had sounded bored as he stretched out his hand.

Fee's heart had sunk.

'I left it at work,' she had told him, raising her eyebrows and looking as casual about the whole thing as she possibly could. 'Stupid or what?'

'No ID, no admittance!'

Fee had pulled back her shoulders and held his gaze.

'Look,' she had said, 'I know you're only doing your job but I'm meeting someone and he'll vouch for me, OK?'

The bouncer had smirked and shaken his head.

Fee had decided that it was a case of do or die.

'Look,' she had said, praying that the fact that she'd put her hair up and piled on the make-up would win the day, 'do I look under age? I mean, get serious!'

The guy had eyed her up and down.

'Two minutes,' he had grunted. 'You get back here with your mate and have him sign you in or you're out, get it?'

Fee's eyes had taken several minutes to become accustomed to the darkness, the strobe lighting and the general press of bodies. She'd been about to give up, conscious as she was of the glances of dancing couples and a group of Year 13s from school, two of whom were eyeing her up and down as if she'd just crawled out from under a log.

But then she'd seen him, leaning nonchalantly against the horseshoe-shaped bar, sipping a drink and chatting to a couple of guys.

'Hi!' She had been grateful that in the dim light he wouldn't be able to see her burning cheeks.

'You came!' She caught the note of surprise in his voice. 'Drink?'

She had nodded and touched his arm.

'Listen – crazy situation, I know, but the guy on the door wants you to vouch for me.'

His two mates had smirked and one of them muttered something in Dean's ear.

'Leave it out!'

He'd taken Fee's arm and pushed his empty glass across the bar.

'No sweat!' he had grinned, lightly planting a kiss on her forehead as he did so. 'Are you telling me he thought you were under age?'

Fee had nodded.

'Dumb, eh?'

'So how old are you?' Dean had asked after he'd scribbled his signature by her name in the book by the door.

'Nineteen,' she'd said lightly, crossing her fingers behind her back and assuring herself that she'd go to confession next week. 'Nearly,' she added, by way of moderating the lie a little.

'Just a babe!' he'd teased. 'Come on, there's a great band downstairs in the Cauldron Bar. Let's give it a whirl!'

Lying in bed, staring up at the ceiling, she knew she should have told the truth about her age from the outset, but at the time, she couldn't see the harm in pretending.

After all, it was him who asked her to the club, and it wasn't as if he hadn't enjoyed being with her.

'I knew the moment I saw you that you were different,' he'd told her as they jigged about on the jam-packed dance floor. 'Couldn't take my eyes off you.'

'Why?' Fee had asked. 'It's not like I'm some slender stunning blonde!'

She'd always found it was better to deprecate yourself before anyone got the chance to do it first.

'No,' Dean had agreed and Fee couldn't help feeling a sense of disappointment. 'But you looked real, not all fake and giggly.'

That's when they had started talking properly – about life (which Dean said should be lived to the full every second of every day); about work (which Dean said should only be the means to an end); and about the world (which, according to Dean, was full of rampant, raving capitalists who thought only about making money and looking good).

They had talked for hours and although she couldn't remember all his arguments one thing had stuck in her mind from that very first night.

'You know what gets up my nose?' he'd commented halfway through the evening. 'Plastic people living plastic lives and pretending to be something they're not.'

He had waved his hand round the room.

'Take this lot,' he'd said. 'A load of airheads, interested only in how they look, who's worth networking with, who's got enough money to show them a good time. It sucks!'

He had taken a long gulp of his shandy.

'And in ten years' time, what will they be doing?'

Fee stared, mesmerised, into his hooded eyes.

'I . . .'

'I'll tell you – they'll be working their guts out for a bigger house, faster car, better holiday – and still pretending they're happy!'

He had slammed his glass down on the bar and stood up.

'Which is why I'm off!'

For a moment, Fee had been alarmed. Surely he wasn't just going to walk out on her?

'Off?'

'Travelling,' he said with a grin. 'See the world, bit of work here, bit there – no luggage, no ties!'

'And your parents don't mind?' The instant the words were out she realised how stupid they sounded.

'I'm twenty-two, Fee – they're hardly in a position to mind!' For a moment, Fee had been speechless. She'd guessed he was nineteen at most.

'Besides,' he went on. 'It's their kind of life I'm getting away from – there's more to life than worrying about the stock market and whether you'll get invited to someone's stupid garden party!'

'Tell me about it!' Fee had burst out. 'My lot want to change the way I look . . .'

'Don't let them!' Dean had urged her. 'Just be you. In the end, you is all you've got.'

He slipped an arm lightly round her shoulder and gave her another quick kiss on the cheek. Electric shocks ran through her body and she tipped her head slightly in hope of something rather more lingering. But he was already pushing his way across the dance floor, beckoning to her to follow.

'I'm grabbing something to eat and then crashing out,' he said. 'Early start tomorrow on the building site . . .'

'You're working as a labourer?' To her horror, she could hear her mother's tones in her own voice. 'I mean, that's great!'

She tried to recover her position but could see that Dean was eyeing her suspiciously.

'Why not?' he asked, giving a brief nod to the bouncer on the door and stepping out onto the pavement. 'Do you have a problem with that?'

'Me? 'Course not!' she declared. 'I just meant – well, when you came to the pizzeria, you didn't look scruffy or anything.'

She wanted to add that he was well-spoken and intelligent, but he was already laughing and she realised she had got away with it.

'Day off!' he said. 'Well, I threw a sickie actually. There's only so much hod carrying a guy can take and let's face it, Crowbrook Retail Park is hardly the most scenic part of town! Now then, curry or Chinese?'

She knew she should have gone home at that point – she hadn't told her mother where she was going simply because she hadn't been able to face the volley of questions she knew she'd get. But she didn't go home; she sat in the Golden Pagoda for another hour, drinking in Dean's sexy looks, soaking up everything he said, and wishing that the evening would last forever.

When he finally called her a cab, she couldn't help herself from asking the one question that everyone said you should never, ever ask.

'Shall I see you again?'

He had shrugged.

'Give me your phone number and let's see what pans out!' he had said.

She'd scribbled her mobile number on a scrap of paper and shoved it in his hand.

'Whatever!' she replied, as lightly as she could. 'No sweat!'

She'd been proud of the way she had used his own phrase. Dead sophisticated.

Of course, once she got home, she had had to face the usual tirade from her mother. The 'What time do you call this?' and 'When Louise was your age, she would never have dreamt of going out without telling me...' and 'Those trousers are quite wrong for someone with big hips.' But for once, she hadn't let it get to her. She'd said 'Sorry, Mum,' and 'I guess you're right' and had smiled inwardly to see how much her meek attitude fazed her mother.

'Who were you with anyway?' her mother had demanded.

'Oh, the gang!' Fee had said airily as though she had retinues of friends lining up to spend the evening with her.

No way had she been prepared to tell her mother about

Dean. There was no need; it was none of her business and besides, it would only have given her something else to complain about. Besides, deep down, Fee hadn't thought it would last.

But it had, she thought now, pounding her pillow with her fist in an attempt to get comfortable. Dean had started texting her every day and they would meet at least three times a week – sometimes just for a coffee, sometimes for longer.

And then he took her to his mate's engagement party.

That was where it had happened. She couldn't remember all the details, just that she was disappointed and had felt that frankly, if that was it, she couldn't see why people went so ecstatic about it. It had been over in seconds, but now there might be something – someone – who would last forever. And if there was she'd have to tell her parents.

They would kill her.

If they weren't too busy killing one another, that was, she thought, stifling a yawn. After she'd thrown up the evening before, she had edged her way down the stairs, straining her ears to catch the conversation in the hallway. Why she did it, she couldn't explain even to herself, but it was always the same. If her parents were rowing, if there was any kind of problem in the family, she felt she had to be one step ahead, had to know exactly what was going on.

Of course, at first it had been all tinkling laughter and exclamations of disbelief.

'I mean, honestly, Max – can you see me bothering with a kid hardly out of school, when I've got this gorgeous woman to come home to?' That was her father, his over-accentuated plummy tones telling Fee just how much he was acting a part.

'I have to say, Max darling, that it's all part of the territory – it comes with being married to a highly successful, incredible hulk!'

Fee had wanted to throw up all over again as she listened to her mother's girlish giggles.

When Max had begun insisting he'd have to leave and get back to London, she had nipped back up the stairs and peered cautiously over the landing banister. As the front door shut, the mood had changed.

'How could you be so stupid? Flirting with a kid hardly older than your own daughter!'

'If you were a proper wife, I wouldn't need to!'

'If I had a man who had actually grown up and become an adult—'

'By grown up, I suppose you mean hard and driven and totally lacking in any kind of fun!'

'You said you were in Spain—'

'So I came home a day early – is there a law against it?'

And so it went on. She should have gone back to her room right then, left them to sort out their own mess. But she had found herself standing at the kitchen door, watching their pinched faces and gritted teeth as they laid into one another.

'Stop it!'

They had turned, and the expressions on their faces were precisely what she had known they would be. Her mother glared at her in irritation; her father's face took on that pleading, little boy lost look.

'Fee, darling!' He took a step towards her and stretched out his hand. 'You believe me, don't you?'

'Believe what?'

'That I was just out having a bit of fun – nothing shameful, nothing underhand. Mummy doesn't seem to understand that in the acting profession—'

'Oh, I understand well enough!' her mother had interjected. 'I understand that you are a two-timing, self-seeking—

'Mum!' Fee had been amazed to hear the sternness of her own voice. 'Leave it! If Dad says it was nothing, it was nothing, OK?'

She might have gone on, might have done what she'd done for years; stuck by her father, sworn that black was white, told her mother that it was all her fault.

But suddenly, something had stopped her. Whether it had been the expression on her father's face – that look of quiet confidence, of muted triumph, the imperceptible nod of the head that told that he knew that, yet again, she'd bale him out; or whether it was the collapse of her mother's meticulously made-up face into a look of undisguised, abandoned misery, she didn't know.

She had walked across the kitchen to where her mother was leaning against the draining board, taken her hand and turned to face her father.

'So it was nothing, Dad, is that right?'

'Absolutely! I knew I could rely on you to make your mother see sense!'

'See, Mum? Nothing. So what Dad's really saying is that we're nothing.' She glared at her father. 'The shame we feel, the fact that my mates all know what he's doing, the way we have to pretend year in, year out that we're a happy family when we're not – all that's nothing!'

For an instant, you could have heard a pin drop in the kitchen. Fee's father had stared at her, open-mouthed, struck speechless by words he hadn't dreamed he would hear. Her mother's expression had hardly changed, but Fee had heard her swallow hard and felt the momentary tightening of her grip on Fee's hand.

To his credit, her father had recovered his composure very quickly.

'Darling, what nonsense!' he had cried. 'You and Mum – you are everything to me! OK, so I was misguided to take Sasha . . .'

'Don't mention that girl's name in this house!' her mother had snapped.

' . . . to take a young girl out to supper,' he had gone on smoothly. 'I'm a big softie, that's all – felt sorry for the kid . . .'

'Don't give me that!' Fee's mother had shouted. 'I was the one who thought up that story for you, remember? This is the second time you've done this to me and . . .'

The rest of their railing had gone over Fee's head. She had stared at her father and in an instant, she knew. Her

114

mother really thought that this was only the second time her dad had been unfaithful. They had stood, father and daughter, gazes locked. And it had been Fee who dropped her eyes first.

Slowly she had walked out of the room. What would have been the point of staying? There was nothing she could do. It was too late. If she'd told the truth at the very beginning, told her mother about Astrid, and then about the Danish girl whose name she forgot, and Ingrid from Sweden, Mum would have given up work and given up au pair girls and stayed at home, and then they would have been happy like Scarlett's parents.

It was, she thought now, giving up any attempt at getting back to sleep, all her own fault.

* * *

'And now it's time to catch up with the early morning news in your neck of the woods!'

Lyall flicked the volume switch on the TV remote control with one hand and spooned Rice Krispies into his mouth with the other. Normally, he'd be lying in bed until the last possible minute and then sprinting to school (or not as the mood took him) with a slice of toast to eat on the run.

But today he actually wanted to get there and he wanted to get there early. If he could give Mrs Faber the camera film, she might get the pictures developed before the end of school.

115

'*Reports are coming in of a confirmed case of meningococcal meningitis at Bishop Andrew School in Harpleton . . .*'

Lyall's spoon fell with a clatter into his cereal bowl as he stared at the TV screen. As the newsreader spoke, the camera panned in a shot of the Bishop Andrew school sign.

'*For the sixteen-year-old girl, who has been admitted to Harpleton General Hospital, the next twenty-four hours will be critical . . .*'

'She's critical – don't tell the boy!' The whispered words echoed in Lyall's head as if they had been spoken yesterday.

The TV camera switched to scenes of ambulances pulling into the forecourt of the A&E department.

'*. . . last month a six-year-old pupil at St Saviour's Primary School was admitted to Harpleton General Hospital with the disease but has now made a full recovery. Doctors hope that . . .*'

Lyall zapped the Off button and flung the remote control onto the table.

Candy hadn't recovered. Candy had died. She'd died because he did as he was told. She died because he hadn't run for help soon enough.

If he hadn't been so good, if he hadn't been obedient . . .

'You're up and dressed early!' His foster mother ambled into the kitchen in her dressing gown, stifling a yawn with one hand and giving him a friendly punch with the other. 'And you've eaten!'

She gestured to the empty cereal bowl on the table and it was then that Lyall realised it was shuddering in time to the rhythmic beating of his fist on the table.

Maddy slipped into the chair next to his and laid a hand gently on his arm.

'What's wrong, Lyall?' They always asked that question when he began to get physical and he never told them the real answer. 'Is it about us? The move?'

'Get real!' he snapped. 'What do I care what you do?'

The pain that darted across Maddy's pale face took even him by surprise and a sharp stab of guilt made him swallow hard.

'Sorry,' he said. 'I . . .'

What could he say? I want my sister back? I want another chance? I didn't mean for her to die? I didn't mean to make you want to get rid of me?

No. There was nothing to say.

'It's OK,' she said, smiling at him and rubbing her forehead wearily. 'And Lyall, I promise we will work something out. Something good. OK?'

He shrugged, pushed back his chair and grabbed the camera bag that was hanging over the back of his chair.

'You're not off already, surely?' Maddy asked, standing up. 'It's only five to eight.'

'I want to get to school early so Mrs Faber can get the film developed,' he told her, pulling the camera from its bag. 'I'll bring the pictures home so you can see them.'

He looked at her anxiously. She seemed odd this morning; like someone who'd woken up and found themselves in a strange place. Maybe she was realising that she didn't want to get rid of him. Maybe she wished she could turn the clock back.

'The pictures won't be that good,' he added hastily, 'but I can keep practising.'

'I'm sure they'll be great,' Maddy said, turning on the tap and filling the kettle. 'And don't be late back, will you, because Jeff's coming round to . . .'

' . . . to give me my marching orders? To tell me I've outstayed my welcome yet again?'

So much for thinking that she was having second thoughts.

'No, not that!' Maddy didn't usually snap and the tone of her voice made Lyall stop dead in his tracks. 'He's got some ideas – things we could do to make it all work out and . . .'

'OK, I'll be back by five!'

Well done, Lyall, very co-operative. Good lad. People like it when you respond well.

'Thanks!' To his surprise, Maddy stepped towards him and planted a kiss on this cheek. To his even greater surprise, he quite liked it.

'Are you going to watch the news?' he asked suddenly, his hand on the back door handle.

Maddy frowned.

'I wasn't – why? Anything special on?'

'Something about our school,' he said. 'Gotta go now!'

And with that he slammed the door and shot out of the back gate.

She'd see the news and she'd know. Maybe. He wasn't sure exactly why he wanted her to know. She'd worry, that much was certain; worry that he'd get meningitis, worry that she wouldn't know what to do and then he'd die.

Worry that she couldn't possibly leave him . . .

He didn't want her to worry and he didn't want her to feel anxious about him.

Much.

★ ★ ★

They were waiting for him, just as he'd known they would be. Jay squared his shoulders, took a deep breath and fingered the two five-pound notes in his trouser pocket.

He'd been in two minds about whether to mention the subject of money to his grandmother again that morning; he honestly didn't think he could have coped with another outburst. But when he had gone downstairs, half asleep because he'd already been up two hours trying to finish the English essay, his nan was already at the breakfast table, munching her way through a slice of toast and honey.

And on the table was her pension book and a wad of notes.

'Toast's in the toaster, dear!' she had greeted him breezily. 'And didn't you say you wanted some cash?'

Jay had been so amazed that for a moment he didn't reply.

'I found my pension book in the freezer with all this money,' she had said, wagging a finger at him. 'Jay, you really must be more careful when you tidy up!'

He hadn't bothered to defend himself. He had been too relieved to see the money.

'I just need ten pounds, Nan,' he had told her. 'I'll pay you back tonight – I'll go to the cash point.'

His gran had picked up the notes and frowned at them.

'Now – which one is it – the blue one or the brown one?'

He had blanked his mind to the infantile question and merely grabbed two five-pound notes and stuffed them into his pocket. Throughout breakfast, he had talked nineteen to the dozen about anything and everything he could think of, just to ward off the possibility of hearing her say something else that simply didn't make sense. To his relief, she seemed perfectly normal, until he mentioned the Town Fair and his idea of seeing if there were any jobs going over the weekend.

'The Fair!' she cried. 'Your mum loved the Fair – every year she'd insist on going, right from when she was a little thing.'

She laughed.

'Mind you, so did I!' Her eyes sparkled and for a minute, she looked ten years younger.

'Not those awful roller coaster things, of course,' she went on. 'But the carousels and the coconut shies – do they still have those? – and the dodgems. Do you know, once I took Barbara on the . . .'

She had gone on and on, chatting away, and even though Jay watched her like a hawk, she didn't do anything bizarre. She even put her money neatly away in her purse and slipped it back into her handbag.

'Everything's going to be fine,' he kept telling himself on the way to school and even now, waiting to cross the busy main road, and seeing Matt and Rick waiting for him at the school gate, he felt upbeat. He'd pay them off and in future he wouldn't be so dumb, wouldn't get himself into a situation where they could get one over him.

'There you are! £5 each, OK?'

Rick snatched both notes and shoved one into Matt's outstretched hand. To Jay's surprise, they backed away from him at once.

'And don't expect any more!' Jay knew before he'd uttered the second syllable that he had made a big mistake. The shove from Rick nearly knocked him off his feet and he staggered backwards, only just missing Matt's swipe at his shin with his steel-toed boot.

'Don't get lippy with us, Squirt!' Jay flinched as a glob of spit landed on his neck. 'And keep your distance – we don't want any of your filthy germs!'

'What do . . . ?' Jay stopped, the question unfinished. No way was he about to engage in conversation with them.

'Don't you know?' Matt was clearly enjoying himself. 'That girl in your class – the swot with the long black hair—'

'Reena? What about her?'

'She's the one that's got it!' Rick said with relish.

'Got what? What are you on about?'

'Meningitis!' Matt interjected. 'I know, because my dad's a porter at the hospital.'

'And you're hanging around with her every lunch hour,' snarled Rick. 'So keep your distance, right?'

His words floated over Jay's head. Reena sick? With meningitis? That was awful. He tried to ignore the wave of relief that washed over him, because he knew that all his thoughts ought to be for her.

But if Matt and Rick were scared of germs, and if he could just perpetuate the story that he was forever seeing Reena, they'd steer clear of him.

'I'll go and see her at the hospital tonight then!'

He began walking away and Matt and Rick didn't follow him.

It was when he reached the double doors into the Main Block that he spotted a group of Reena's friends.

'Is it true?' he asked Sumitha. 'About Reena?'

She nodded.

'She's in hospital,' she whispered. 'With meningitis.'

'There's a special assembly, Mrs Faber said . . . nurse coming to talk . . . letters to take home . . .'

The babble washed around Jay but he didn't take any of it in. Another thought had just hit him. Meningitis was catching. And he'd been with Reena just three days before in Science Club.

And so had Fiona.

What if . . . ? Oh God, yesterday Fiona had missed Science Club because she felt sick.

Puking was a sure sign.

What if she ended up in hospital like Reena?

His eyes darted round the forecourt. There was no sign of her.

He had to find her. Make sure she was OK.

He could pretend he was worried about the competition. He would never dare tell her how much he fancied her.

6

'Now I don't want any of you to worry,' Mr Carter, the head was saying. 'The chances of this spreading are very small indeed, but just to be sure...'

Lyall let his words drift over his head as he stared at the leaflet they'd all been given as they filed into assembly.

'What is meningitis?'

He flipped over the page.

And there she was, staring up out of the page into his face. Blonde hair, flushed cheeks. And the spots.

'The leaflet will tell you all you need to know... spot the symptoms...' Mr Carter's voice had taken on a brisk, matter-of-fact tone.

'My neck hurts, Lyall... turn the light off, Lyall... I'm sleepy...'

He'd thought it was good when she went to sleep. Mum always said she liked them best when they were sleeping. So he hadn't bothered to try waking her. Even when the spots came, he just rubbed on some nappy cream and went on playing with his tiddlywinks on the lino floor. He knew Mum would be home soon and she'd be so proud of him for getting his sister off to sleep. She might even get him fish and chips as a reward.

He'd got fish and chips but not from Mum. The lady with the red hair had given him some.

He hadn't eaten them.

They hadn't tasted right.

He'd wanted the ones his mum bought.

He'd wanted Mum.

He still wanted her.

'Get a move on, dopey!' Someone's elbow jabbed into his side. He hadn't noticed that Mr Carter had stopped talking, that assembly was over. He scrambled to his feet. She'd be... He paused, causing the person behind him to swear under his breath. She'd be thirty-four now, his mum. She could be married, have other kids, be living in a swish house...

'Mum's going away for a bit... you'll see her again soon.'

But he hadn't. He hadn't seen her for ages. Even when they found her in Spain with that bloke and she'd been to court and everything, he'd only seen her a couple of times and even then, they'd never been alone together. The first time, she'd hugged him and stroked his hair and been ever so nice but not like her real self at all. And the second time...

But he wouldn't think about the second time.

'Ah, Lyall, the very person I wanted to see!' Mrs Faber's upbeat tones broke in on his thoughts. 'How did the photography go?'

'Great!' he replied, unzipping his bag and handing her the exposed film. 'Well, I mean, it was fun,' he gabbled, still trying to push the memories out of his brain, 'but they're probably useless!'

'Why do you do this, Lyall?' Mrs Faber frowned.

'Do what, Miss?'

'Run yourself down all the time,' she went on. 'You've an artist's eye; I'm sure the pictures will be great. And if they're not – well, you'll just take more, won't you?'

She tossed the film in the air and caught it, grinning at him.

'Right! I'll get these to the one hour photo place down the road and then we'll see what's what!'

She eyed him curiously.

'Are you OK?'

He didn't answer. He just walked away.

She used to do that. His mum used to take the keys and throw them up in the air.

'Catch, Lyall!'

He never could. She always caught them first.

And she always laughed.

'I'll be back!' she would call as she locked them in.

But she'd lied.

She hadn't come back.

Ever.

The prison people let her go in the end, but she hadn't come to get him.

He'd heard them say in the children's home that after a while, the boy would forget.

He wished they had been right. Forgetting would have been so much easier.

* * *

'So what about your dad, Fee? What's happening?'

'Is he really – well, you know – with that girl?'

'It's in all the papers this morning...'

Fee's heart sank. She had thought she'd got away with it, thought that everyone was too stewed up about poor Reena Banerjee to worry about her father.

Some hope. She'd only been in the queue for lunch for half a second when the questions started.

'It's all something about nothing,' she replied with what she hoped was a casual shrug of the shoulders. 'Just the press looking for a story that isn't there.'

She hated herself for following in her mother's footsteps, but what choice did she have? She could hardly tell them the truth; it wasn't the sort of thing you wanted the world to know. For the first time in her life, she began to see things from her mother's point of view, began to think that, just possibly, pretending was no bad thing. Not if it shut people up and got them off your back for a while.

'So is he going to sue the newspapers?' Tanya asked, eyeing her closely. 'People do, you know, if it's all really a lie.'

'Shut it!' Scarlett glared at Tanya and gave Fee's arm an encouraging squeeze. 'It's none of our business.'

Fee threw her a grateful smile but Scarlett's attempts at changing the subject had fallen on deaf ears.

'My mum read in the paper this morning that Sasha Sandrino says they've been in love for months!'

That was Verity Fisher, clearly relishing her role as purveyor of bad news.

'I know!' someone else chipped in. 'And on breakfast TV, they showed pictures of...'

Whether it was the memories of the past twelve hours, or the revolting smell of what the school caterers called Hungarian Goulash, Fee didn't know, but suddenly she felt the bile rising in her throat and knew beyond all possible doubt that she was going to be sick.

Again.

She only just made it to the loo in time. When she'd finished retching and heaving, she staggered out of the cubicle and straight into Scarlett.

'Fee, are you OK? They don't mean it you know – they're just glad to have something else to think about after all this talk of meningitis and—'

She paused, her hand clamped to her mouth.

'Oh my God!' she gasped. 'You don't think . . . you're not . . . I mean, have you got a headache? Stiff neck?'

'Don't you start!' she muttered. 'Jason's asked me three times whether I'm better. I wish!'

Fee tried to smile but it didn't work out that way. To her horror, she felt her face crumple as a strangled sob escaped from her lips.

'Fee? What is it? What's wrong – is it your dad?'

'No, I don't give a damn about my dad right now!' She felt too ill and too scared to care about anything or anyone except what was going on in her body.

She dumped her bag beside the basins and turned on the taps.

'What then?' Scarlett slipped an arm around Fee's shoulder and glared at an Eighth year who was staring at them in curiosity.

'I . . . it's . . .' Fee paused as the girl washed her hands in the adjacent basin and then, with a reluctant backward glance, left the cloakroom.

'It hasn't come.'

'You don't mean . . . oh, Fee! You're not . . .' Scarlett left the word hanging in the air.

'I don't know,' Fee sobbed, fumbling in her bag for a tissue. 'I mean, I'm two weeks late and . . .'

'Two weeks!' Scarlett gasped. 'So have you done a pregnancy test?'

Fee shook her head.

'Then you must! At once!' Scarlett ordered. 'I mean, let's face it, Fee – you've got to know one way or the other. The sooner you know the sooner you can get it sorted.'

'Sorted? Oh sure, my parents will sort me once and for all if they—'

'Not if you get rid of it!'

For a moment, Fee felt as if her heart had stopped beating. She couldn't do that. Never. Not ever. No matter what. She stared at Scarlett and opened her mouth to protest.

'I couldn't . . . oh, God, I'm going to be sick again!'

She didn't hear her phone ringing over the sound of her own retching and the noisy flushing of the ancient cistern. But when she emerged, sweating and wobbly, from the cubicle, she found Scarlett clutching Fee's phone to her ear, a puzzled frown on her face.

'She can't come right now . . . what? Where is she? At school, of course – where else? Shall I . . . ?'

'Give that to me!' Fee grabbed the phone from Scarlett.

'Hello! Hello!' She stared at the screen. 'They've gone! Who was it?'

'Some guy,' Scarlett shrugged. 'He said "Hi, Fee, is that you?" but then when he realised it wasn't, he rang off. Rude or what?'

'I don't believe it!' Fee sobbed. 'It must have been Dean. I've waited for days and now—'

'So ring him back, dippy!' smiled Scarlett.

Fee punched keys on her phone.

'Withheld!' she groaned. 'I can't call him.'

'You must have his number,' Scarlett insisted. 'You've been going out with the guy for weeks.'

Fee said nothing.

'You don't have his number?' Scarlett's eyes widened. 'What kind of a relationship do you call that?'

'You don't understand,' Fee retorted. 'He's a free spirit, he doesn't like being tied down or hounded.'

Even as she said it, she realised just how hollow it sounded.

'And you swallowed that one? God, Fee, I'd have credited you with more sense.'

Fee wanted to protest, but she didn't have the energy. She hadn't eaten chocolate all day; lunch was just salad and salad doesn't make you sick.

She had to be pregnant.

'Right!' Scarlett picked up Fee's bag and passed it to her as the Registration bell shrilled in the corridor. 'First, we get you a testing kit. When are you seeing Dean again?'

Fee sighed.

'Never, probably. We sort of . . . well, he broke it off. On Sunday.'

Scarlett stared at her.

'He broke it off? Why?'

'See, I told him I was nineteen, and then . . .'

'You did what? Are you mad?'

Scarlett pushed Fee out into the crowded corridor and glanced at her watch.

'I had to lie to get into The Melting Pot,' Fee gabbled, 'and anyway, it didn't seem that important . . .'

'And then he found out that you're only sixteen?'

Fee nodded.

'I had to tell him – I mean, what with term starting and me finishing at the pizzeria and stuff. He went ballistic.'

'I bet he did!' Scarlett nodded, as they turned into the Science block corridor. 'And that was after you'd . . . well, you know, done . . . ?'

Fee nodded. Scarlett said nothing. She merely shook her head slowly and sighed a lot.

'But don't you see?' Fee urged, wiping her eyes surreptitiously on the back of her hand and allowing a faint glimmer of hope to penetrate her anxiety. 'He's phoned! So he wants to see me again, despite everything! That's good, isn't it?'

'It had better be. But from now on, you're going to have to be dead honest with him!' Scarlett retorted. 'Look, we can't talk now – but promise me you'll get a kit, and you'll talk to Dean.'

Fee bit her lip.

'Promise?' Scarlett repeated sternly.

'I'll try – but . . .'

'But what?'

'I don't know where he lives and . . .'

Scarlett closed her eyes and sighed.

'I've heard it all now,' she said. 'So where does he work?'

Fee's face brightened.

'He said something about . . . Crowbrook! That was it!'

'There you are then!' Scarlett stressed. 'Do it, Fee. Find him, tell him what . . .'

'No – I mean, not till I know for sure!' Fee cried. 'It might all be a false alarm. You said it could be the holiday and I have had twinges and . . .'

'OK, OK,' acknowledged Scarlett. 'It's your life. But deal with it!'

Fee nodded. She would. She could now. Because Dean wouldn't have phoned if he hadn't been missing her dreadfully. He wouldn't have bothered to get in touch unless he wanted to see her again.

She felt almost cheerful. If there was a baby, they could work it out. She wouldn't tie him down; they could go travelling together. People took babies abroad all the time these days.

'And Fee?' Scarlett touched her arm. 'Come to the Fair tonight with the rest of us, yeah?'

Fee knew that Scarlett was trying to say that, no matter what, they were mates.

She smiled.

'OK, then!' she nodded. If things went well, if she convinced Dean that she wasn't some dippy kid, he'd go with her to the Fair. Then Scarlett would see that he really did love her.

If she found him.

If he forgave her.

He would. She'd make him.

It would be fine.

Please God.

★ ★ ★

'Leave it out, Miss! I don't want to go and that's it, OK?'

Never in his life had Jay spoken to a teacher that way, but he'd had it with Miss Perry banging on and on about the French exchange.

He had hoped that she'd got the message earlier that afternoon, when she had buttonholed him on the way into English. He had told her then that he wasn't going but would she let it rest?

'Jay, this isn't like you!' she had protested. 'What's wrong – all your enthusiasm seems to have disappeared.'

Jay had shrugged.

'No, Miss – it's just that—'

'Just what, Jason? If there's some sort of problem, we should talk about it. Anything you tell me is confidential and...'

Just for a fleeting instant, he had wanted to pour it all out – to tell her about Nan and the sandwich, and the money and the way she couldn't remember things.

'It's just that my nan . . .'

Even as he had uttered the first few words, he could hear his grandmother's voice as clearly as if she was standing beside him.

'No need to wash our dirty linen in public, Jay!'

How could he say anything? Besides, this morning his nan had been quite like her old self, especially when he'd mentioned that he might pop over to the Fair that evening.

'You go, dear, and have a good time! You deserve it, what with all that hard work the school gives you!'

She'd even offered him a five-pound note to spend.

'Have a go on the coconut shy for me!' she'd giggled. He hadn't had the heart to tell her they didn't have coconut shies any more.

'What about your nan, Jason?' Miss Perry had leaned towards him and lowered her voice as more students piled into the classroom.

'She's not . . .'

It was no good. He couldn't grass on her.

'There's not been any more trouble, has there, Jason? Like before?'

Jay had stared at her. How did she know? No one knew about that, no one at all.

'Like I said, Miss, I don't want to go, OK? Here's my essay!'

He had dumped it on the table and, thankful that too many people were hanging around for Miss Perry to be able to carry on talking, had grabbed a seat in the far corner of the classroom. The double lesson had passed in a blur; he kept thinking about Miss Perry's words and wondering just what she knew. And now, here she was, cornering him as everyone was leaving, going on at him again.

'Jason,' she repeated patiently, 'I know that your grandmother had some problems earlier in the year. But that's OK . . .'

'Oh sure it's OK!' Jay exploded. 'It might be from where you're standing but—'

'She took things, didn't she?' Miss Perry sounded as calm and laid back as if she'd been commenting on the performance of one of her more able students in a drama production. 'From the neighbours?'

He'd read in books about people whose hearts missed a beat or who swore that time stood still. He'd always thought it was just poetic licence. Now he knew it happened.

His chest tightened and he willed himself to think of something, anything, that he could say that would shut the woman up.

'She didn't mean it.'

He had as good as admitted his nan's crime. He felt the colour flooding his cheeks and ran his hand over his face as if he could obliterate the blushing by sheer willpower.

She was saying something but he didn't hear. His mind was filled with the images of that day he got home from the field trip.

'I was all for calling the police . . . after all we've done for her . . . she just walked in as large as life . . .'

Mr Burns from next door had towered over him within minutes of him dumping his suitcase on the hall floor.

' . . . sat herself down as if she owned the place . . . had the audacity to say the sausages were overdone . . .'

'She loves sausages!' The stupid response had just made Mr Burns more angry.

' . . . then we find her marching home with two bottles of the Sainsbury's Chardonnay under her arm . . .'

' . . . not to mention the toffee ice cream we'd got in for our Jodie.'

Mrs Burns had materialised behind her husband, arms akimbo and glowering at Jason as if she suspected him of orchestrating the entire event.

' . . . and to make matters worse, she denies all knowledge of it . . good thing we'd invited the Fletchers and the Newmans over, 'cos they'll vouch for what she did . . .'

Of course, he'd apologised, made up some excuse about his nan being very forgetful because of the antibiotics she was on (which was a laugh, since his grandmother had always blatantly refused to take any medicine the doctor gave her and would just tip them down the sink). He'd gone to Sainsbury's and tried to buy more wine to make it up to them, but no one would serve him because they said he was under age. He'd got the ice cream though – four tubs of it.

The Burns had just grunted and said that in future he'd best not go gallivanting but stay at home and watch the old fool.

So he had. But now Miss Perry, who probably lived in a house full of sane, intelligent people who never forgot to turn the taps off, was digging it all up again.

'Who told you...?'

Miss Perry smiled apologetically.

'You get to hear a lot of gossip when you're a teacher,' she replied tactfully. 'The point is, are things bad again? Has she...?'

'No, she's fine!' Even he could hear how false and flat his words sounded.

'But you still don't feel you can leave her, right?'

He didn't nod. But then he didn't shake his head either.

'Got to go, Miss,' he gabbled. 'Things to do.'

She didn't push it. She just nodded briefly, picked up her books and pushed open the door with her foot.

'Going to the Fair this weekend, Jason?' she asked, clearly trying to lighten the atmosphere. 'It seems the entire school will be there!'

The Fair! He hadn't given it a thought all afternoon and now it was nearly four o'clock and if he didn't rush, he'd miss Fiona and never have the chance to ask her to go with him.

'It would do you good, Jason,' added Miss Perry, taking his silence as denial. 'Forget your problems for a bit...'

'Yes, Miss!'

He caught the pleased expression on her face as he scooted past her and down the stairs. If Fiona said yes, if he could spend a whole evening with her, think of witty things to say and buy her candy floss and stuff, then maybe she'd see that he was an OK guy.

Who was he kidding? She hadn't been over the moon with him that morning; in fact, whenever he asked if she was OK, she told him to stop acting like an old woman. Besides, everyone knew that girls wanted to go out with guys who were taller than them.

Everyone was taller than him.

But he'd ask her anyway. She could only say no.

Which, of course, she most certainly would.

7

'Shopping for the third millennium! Crowbrook Retail Park – the biggest mall in the Midlands!'

Fee watched the bus disappear in a cloud of dust behind the huge hoarding and scanned the half finished shopping complex. Only a few of the stores had been completed but nearly all of them had their roofs on. But at the far corner, scaffolding still towered against the skyline and she could see brickies clambering up ladders, their shouts wafting across to her on the freshening wind.

The closer she got to the site, the more nervous she felt. All the way over on the bus she had rehearsed what she would say to him and she was still no nearer having the words in her head. She caught sight of her reflection in one of the new plate glass windows of Whistles and wished she had ignored Scarlett's advice and gone home to change.

'No way!' Scarlett had protested when Fee had suggested it. 'If this thing is going to work out, he has to accept you as you really are!'

She had eyed Fee solemnly.

'Besides, if he loves you, what you're wearing won't matter!'

If he loves you ... ! But of course he loved her – he'd said so, hadn't he?

'I like your style . . . you make me laugh . . . sexy thing!'

That last phrase had delighted her – she had never believed you could be plump and tall and sexy as well.

'You do love me though, don't you?' Remembering the note of desperation in her voice that evening at the party, she cringed inwardly as she picked her way along the uneven path to the building site.

He had taken so long to reply that she had repeated the question.

'I guess I must do,' he had murmured, nuzzling her neck.

She wished he had sounded more certain, wished that he hadn't changed the subject quite so quickly. But then, guys were like that, weren't they? Embarrassed by the power of their own feelings – that's what she'd read in a magazine once.

'Shops aren't open yet, doll!'

She was jolted out of her reverie by the sound of laughter, and looked up to see two young guys hanging off the scaffolding and ogling her.

She pulled herself up to her full height.

'I'm looking for Dean Rogers,' she called, hoping that she sounded authoritative. 'Is he around?'

The fatter of the two men cupped his right hand to his mouth.

'Dean! Your luck's changed, mate!'

Fee followed his gaze. Dean was poised halfway up a ladder, a hod full of bricks across his shoulder.

She lifted her hand and waved, trying desperately to look relaxed and unconcerned.

Dean caught her eye. He turned and continued walking up the ladder.

'Hey, mate!' The younger of the two guys on the scaffolding called out. 'If you're not coming, we'll 'ave 'er!'

Fee glared at him disparagingly. To her relief, Dean had dumped the bricks and was scooting back down the ladder.

'You're a dark horse, Dean!' the fat one laughed as Dean came towards her. 'Cradle snatching, aren't you?'

Fee could have cried. That did it. He didn't need reminding that she was just a kid, not now, not in front of his workmates.

'What the hell are you doing here?' His greeting was hardly laden with warmth.

'I just had to see you!' she began, keeping her voice as low as she could. 'We need to talk.'

At least he didn't tell her to get lost. He just stood there, staring into her face, neither speaking nor smiling.

'I'm sorry I lied about my age,' she gabbled on. 'I knew they'd throw me out of the night club if I admitted the truth and I just wanted to spend time with you.'

She knew Scarlett would have told her that she was coming on too strong, but she didn't care. She just had to make him see sense.

'But after that,' retorted Dean. 'You could have told me the truth the next day. But no – you let me think you were nineteen for seven whole weeks, Fee!'

'But does it make any difference?'

For the briefest moment, his hand brushed hers – then

he averted his gaze, and kicked at some loose stones with his boot.

'Yes,' he said shortly. 'Yes it does.'

She could feel the tears welling up in her eyes.

'So you never loved me after all!' Her voice broke.

Dean gave a short laugh.

'You don't get it, do you?' he replied. 'It's because I do – did – love you, that it matters.'

She opened her mouth to speak but he was already turning away.

'I've got to get back to work,' he said. 'And I'm sure you've got homework to do!'

The taunting tone of his voice cut through her like a knife.

'Dean, wait!' She could sense that the guys on the scaffolding had downed tools and were watching, but she didn't care. 'Look, I was wrong, OK? I know that now and I'm sorry. But I'm still the same person that you . . . that I was. The date on my birth certificate doesn't alter that.'

She took a deep breath and charged on.

'Can't we just carry on like we were?'

He turned to her wearily.

'What? Until the next time you lie to me?'

'I'll never lie to you again, I promise.' Unless something happened pretty soon, she'd be telling him a whole lot of truths he probably didn't want to hear.

'You said you'd take me to the Fair!' She realised at once how petulant that sounded. Petulant and childish – just what she didn't want to seem.

But to her relief, he smiled.

'I'd forgotten about the Fair,' he admitted. 'Well . . .'

'Dean, mate – these shops need building before the next millennium, you know!'

He glanced over to his mates.

'Coming!' He leaned towards Fee. 'Well, let's just see what pans out, OK?'

'You mean, you'll come to the Fair . . .'

'I mean, let's see what pans out!' There was a note of impatience in his voice. 'It's on tonight, yes?'

She nodded.

'It's on all weekend and I'll be there each night,' she said. 'I'll be hanging out by the scary rides! If I see you, I see you! 'Bye!'

She turned and walked away as briskly as the uneven ground would let her. She didn't look back.

She didn't want to risk him seeing the tears pouring down her face.

★ ★ ★

They were waiting for him when he got home. Patrick and Maddy were sitting in their usual chairs in the lounge, Jeff was sprawled on the sofa surrounded by brightly coloured folders and piles of papers in Rexel sleeves.

'Lyall! Good to see you!' Jeff jumped to his feet and slapped Lyall on the back. 'And I hear you've got good news!'

It was the forced heartiness that Lyall hated, the 'we're

all mates together' business that didn't really mean a thing.

'Good news? You mean, being chucked out is meant to make me dance for joy?'

To Jeff's credit, his expression didn't alter.

'No, silly – this GCSE Sculpture thing! Sounds fascinating – and art is your best subject, right?'

Lyall nodded. So they'd told him. That had to mean they were proud of him. That was good.

'Have you seen the pictures yet?' Maddy asked. He noticed that she looked more tired and pallid than ever. Perhaps it was guilt.

He nodded again.

'Mrs Faber says they are really good,' he stressed. 'She wants me to work on lots of ideas.'

He didn't add that the art teacher's idea involved sculpted figures rising from an empty grave (supported by a wire, she said, though how that would work he didn't have a clue). He'd had to pretend that the grave pictures were just ways of using up the film.

'I don't think so, Lyall,' she said with a wry smile. 'I think it's your soul speaking.' Like he said, she could be dead weird.

'That's terrific!' Jeff sat down again and picked up his papers. 'Can I see them sometime?'

Lyall nodded. Mrs Faber had wanted to hang on to them for a bit, but she'd promised he could have them by next Monday.

Not that he'd probably be here on Monday. He'd probably have been chucked out by then.

'Now then,' Jeff said briskly, 'we've lots to discuss. First of all—'

'Just say it like it is!' Lyall burst out. 'They're moving house, they don't want me to go with them, and you've been lumbered with deciding what to do with me!'

Jeff shook his head.

'It's not like that, Lyall,' he began calmly. 'I've had a chat with Maddy and Patrick and we've decided that they must tell you the truth.'

Lyall frowned.

'They don't like me any more.' It was a statement, not a question.

'Lyall, we love you!' Patrick leaned towards him, his face flushed. 'That's why we didn't tell you everything straight away. We didn't want to . . .'

He faltered and looked to Jeff for support. Maddy got up and walked to the window, her back to all of them.

'Lyall, Maddy is not well.' Jeff rested a hand on Lyall's knee momentarily. 'She's not well at all.'

Somewhere in the pit of Lyall's stomach a knot began forming.

'What sort of not well?' he muttered.

Jeff took a deep breath.

'Maddy has cancer, Lyall,' he said softly.

The knot tightened. A chill rippled through Lyall's body and he wrapped his arms round his chest.

'That's why she and Patrick are moving. Maddy wants to be with her mum and sister back in Scotland.'

'But I can go there too,' he cried. 'I won't be in the way,

and I'll do more to help and . . .'

Jeff held up a hand.

'Lyall, it's not practical. You'd have to change schools and make new friends, and . . .'

'That's OK . . .'

'No!' Jeff interjected. 'You see, it would only be a few months and then . . .'

His voice faded but Lyall had heard enough. Everyone in the room began to go blurry; Jeff's voice was a vague hum above the thundering of Lyall's heart.

'Maddy!' Someone was shouting Maddy's name. They shouldn't do that. Sick people had to be kept quiet.

'A few months and then . . .'

Maddy was going to die.

He wouldn't let it happen. Not again. No way. He'd save her. He'd show them he was an OK guy to be around ill people. He was grown up now, not a kid any longer.

'Maddy!' She turned and he realised that he was the one doing the shouting.

'I'm so sorry, love,' she said.

'But you can get operations,' Lyall insisted. 'Drugs and stuff, that make it go away.'

Jeff sighed.

'For some people, that works,' he said. 'But for Maddy, it's too late. It's gone too far, it's . . .'

'Don't!' Patrick jumped to his feet and began pacing the room.

And Lyall saw that he was crying.

That was when he realised that this was for real. This

wasn't going to change, no matter how good he tried to be, no matter what schemes he came up with to persuade them to take him with them.

Maddy was going to die.

She couldn't do this to him. What had she done – she didn't smoke, she hardly ever had a drink; so how come she was ill?

'There's this lovely lady, Lyall, who looks after older teenagers like you . . .'

'You'd be able to phone and write to Maddy and Patrick and . . .'

'This lady, Lyall – Mrs MacDonald – she's got another couple of lads with her right now, your sort of age and . . .'

' . . . give you more independence and . . .'

The conversation lapped round him.

He knew why they were going to Scotland. They didn't trust him. That was the bottom line. They wanted to be shot of him because he wasn't to be trusted around ill people.

'Please don't go!'

He had never begged anyone for anything before.

'We have to, Lyall,' his foster father replied gently. 'Maddy needs her mother and sister at a time like this. You have to understand.'

The knot unravelled itself in his stomach as the daggers took charge.

She didn't need him. Just two people she only got to see twice a year. So much for being one of the family.

'Suit yourself!' he shouted. 'Won't matter much anyway,

'cos I'll probably be dead too!'

'Lyall, no!' Maddy spun round and moved towards him.

He hurled the meningitis leaflet and the letter from the headmaster at her feet.

'I hope I do get it and I hope I die too!'

Maddy's eyes scanned the leaflet.

'Oh, Lyall! I had no idea. That must be so hard for you – remembering Candy and . . . you must feel . . .'

He wasn't going to hang about to talk about feelings. That's what they always did, expected you to chat on about how it felt, and what you thought you could do about it.

There wasn't anything he could do about it. It might be his life, but he was the last person ever to get a say in it.

He stormed out of the room, slamming the door with all the force he could muster.

'Lyall, come back!' Jeff was hard on his heels. 'I know how awful this is for you, but I promise, we can sort things out.'

Oh sure they could. And they would. He knew that. He wasn't stupid. But right now, he couldn't face it.

Right now, he had to get his head round things in his own way and in his own time.

Right now, he had to be alone.

And yet, deep down inside, he knew that being alone was the last thing on earth he wanted.

★ ★ ★

Jay glanced at the kitchen clock for the tenth time in as many minutes. Where was she? He knew Fridays was her day for going to the afternoon bingo with Beryl, but she was always back by five.

And now it was gone six o'clock.

He pulled the saucepan of baked beans off the hob and turned off the gas. She'd be nattering round at Beryl's house; well, he'd have to go and fetch her, or he'd be late getting to the Fair. Of course, he never managed to catch up with Fiona after school, but her mate Scarlett had told him that a whole gang of them were going to meet there at seven.

'I guess you better come and meet her there if it's urgent!' she had said airily. Jay had been quite chuffed to be included.

He flicked on the latch on the front door and scooted down the road to Beryl's house. He had rung the bell three times and rattled the letter box endlessly before the door finally opened.

'Jason dear! Sorry, I was just on the phone to my grandson, you know the one I told you about, up at Durham university he is, doing ever so well, well I knew he would because he's got my late hubby's brains you see and...'

Jay knew that if he didn't interrupt, Beryl's verbal diarrhoea would carry on for hours.

'Is Nan with you?'

Beryl stopped in mid-flow and frowned.

'Ellen? No she is not. I'm pleased to say.'

'But the bingo...'

'She didn't come to bingo. Oh, I went to fetch her as

148

usual, and what does she do? Accuses me of taking money from her purse! Calls me a thief! Can you believe it?'

Oh yes, thought Jay, his heart sinking, I can believe it only too easily.

'I'm sure she didn't mean . . .' he began

'Now I know she's your grandmother and it's right you should stick up for her, but she can't be allowed to make accusations like that. It really upset me – I told her she could get herself to bingo.'

'She forgets things . . .' Jay began.

Beryl nodded slowly.

'Now you say that, I can be frank, can't I, dear?' She beckoned him over the threshold.

'I mustn't stop – I need to find . . .'

'Just a second!' Beryl shut the front door firmly. 'I have to confess that lately, Ellen's seemed a bit funny.'

Jay swallowed and tried to look surprised.

'Funny? How do you mean?'

'Well, one day she'll be fine, and then the next she's talking all about someone called Barbara and how she's got to get to the school to meet her, and when I ask her what she's on about, she goes kind of blank and—'

'Barbara was my mum!' He shouldn't have said that. He definitely should have kept his mouth shut.

Beryl's hand flew to her mouth.

'Your mum . . .' course I knew you were on your own with Nan, but she never said . . .'

'She died in a car crash years back,' he said. 'Nan sometimes gets a bit confused and thinks she's still around.'

'And what does the doctor say?'

'Doctor?' Jay looked at her blankly.

'Jason, she needs help,' Beryl said. 'It all falls into place now. When I first moved in, she offered to help me get straight and do you know what she did?'

Jay didn't want to know.

'She started cleaning the window frames with a toothbrush!' she declared. 'Went on about keeping germs away, about Barbara having a weak chest. She's not right.'

'She's fine!' Jay retorted. 'Just a bit tired and stuff. So – you saw her at bingo, right?'

Beryl shook her head.

'No, dear, she never turned up,' she said. 'I guess she was too ashamed to face me after what she'd said. But of course, if I'd realised ...'

'But if she didn't go to bingo, where is she?' Jay said, half to himself.

'She can't have gone far,' Beryl told him, but she didn't sound convinced. 'She'll be back any minute, you'll see.'

She'd better be, Jay thought as he belted back to the house.

'Nan! Nan, are you back?'

The silence echoed around him.

He sped up the stairs and threw open the door to his grandmother's bedroom.

And stopped dead in his tracks.

The bed was covered with yellowing newspaper

cuttings and scattered photographs.

He had to get going, to start looking for his grandmother, but curiosity held him back. He went over to the bed and picked up a photograph.

It was his mum and him – or at least, he guessed it was him. A tiny bundle dressed in a blue Babygro. There were dozens more – him and his mother in the park, feeding the ducks, him with a huge cuddly lion, even one of him lying in bed fast asleep.

As he pulled another photo from the pile, his eyes fell on a newspaper cutting.

'One dead, five injured in motorway pile up!'

He caught his breath. A picture of his mother stared up at him.

'A young mother was killed last night when the stolen car she was driving...'

Stolen? It couldn't have been. Nan never said...

'...ploughed cross the central reservation and into the path of an oncoming lorry.'

Wrong again. The lorry had been the one to crash through the barrier. Nan had always said the driver deserved to die, not Barbara.

He scanned his eyes down the page.

'The passenger in the car, Mr Marcus Chapman, escaped with a broken leg, fractured collar bone and cuts to his face and arms...'

So how come his dad had died? People didn't die from broken legs. He must have had internal injuries that they didn't discover till later.

He flicked an eye across the other cuttings on the bed.
'Lorry driver in shock . . .'
'Crash victim leaves 2-year-old son . . .'
'Smash driver had been drinking . . .'
Drinking? Not Mum – that was his father. That was why his mum had been driving – because his father had been the worse for wear. He'd heard the story a dozen times.

He jumped as the front doorbell shrilled. At last! She was back. Impulsively, he grabbed a handful of cuttings, crossed the landing to his bedroom and stuffed them under the mattress. Not too many, just in case his grandmother was with it for once and noticed what he'd done. But something told him there were things he needed to know.

And he wasn't sure just how much of the truth he was likely to get from Nan.

He ran downstairs and yanked open the front door. It wasn't Nan. It was Beryl.

'It just came to me as I was getting the tea,' she began, 'and I thought, I'd better go and tell young Jason right away. So I said to John – you've met John, my husband . . .'

'Tell me what?' asked Jay.

'Your nan,' she went on. 'She said that she didn't give two hoots about the bingo because she was going to the Fair. Said that she went to the Fair every year and she couldn't let the family down by saying no.'

Jay swallowed hard. It all began to make sense. For some reason, she'd started looking at all those photographs and newspaper cuttings and began thinking of Barbara. And what was it she'd said the day before?

'*Your mum loved the Fair – every year she'd insist on going, right from when she was a little thing.*'

'Thanks, Beryl,' he said, turning and grabbing his jacket from the hook on the wall. 'I bet that's where she is.'

'I'd offer to come with you but my fish pie is just browning and . . .'

'I'll be fine!' he said, far more cheerily than he felt. 'She probably thinks we agreed to meet there – my fault for not making things clear!'

No way was he going to have her telling the neighbours that Ellen Rust was a fruit loop. Better take the blame himself.

He slammed the door behind him and headed down the path, dodging in front of Beryl's lumbering bulk. In the far distance he could hear the discordant notes of a fairground organ wafting from the direction of Abbey Park. For a moment, sheer irritation overtook his anxiety for his grandmother's safety.

He shouldn't be scouring the streets for her. He should be going to the Fair to have fun, to find Fiona, not to search for some dippy old lady.

Whenever things went wrong, it was always Nan at the bottom of it.

He'd find her and tell her straight. She had to start concentrating or else.

Or else what, he hadn't a clue.

8

'You can't keep running away, Lyall!'

He'd been aware of the dark blue Mondeo pulling up beside him, known instinctively that it was Jeff, but he'd simply kept on walking.

'Where the hell have you been?'

The car door slammed and Jeff fell into step alongside him.

Lyall said nothing. He could just imagine the expression on the social worker's face if he'd told the truth.

He hadn't meant to go to the vicarage; he had just found himself standing on the step, his finger pressing the brass bell push.

'Oh, it's you! Come in!' The vicar had made it sound as if she'd been expecting him. 'Forgive the mess – The Mothers Union have got a jumble sale tomorrow and they seem to think I'm their own personal warehouse.'

'It's about dying – that's what I've come about.' He'd told himself that there was no point making small talk.

'I thought it might be,' she had said pleasantly. 'Have a seat.'

He remembered thinking that she was being far too nice. That would stop when she knew what he'd done.

'My sister's dead because of me,' he had blurted out. 'That's why my foster mum doesn't want me any more, what with her dying and everything...'

'Why don't you start at the beginning and tell me about it?'

So he had. For what seemed like ages. And in the end, he'd managed to say the one thing he'd been trying to say all along.

'When my foster mum dies, will she see Candy? Will she be able to say sorry to Candy for me?'

'She won't have to.'

The vicar had smiled at him.

'You didn't kill Candy, Lyall. Meningitis killed Candy. What Candy knows is that you did everything in your power to help her – far, far more than any child could have been expected to do.'

Platitudes, thought Lyall. More soft soap.

'But she still died,' he had retorted. 'And I don't get it.'

'Me neither,' she had admitted. 'But I can tell you one thing. Candy would want you to put it behind you and get out in the world and go on doing good things – just like you did for her.'

She'd said a whole lot more than that, more than he could remember now, but one thing stuck in his mind.

'The best way to show love to the dead is to give joy to the living.'

He'd repeated that over and over in his head, and now he thought he got it. So he'd made up his mind.

'Lyall, are you listening to me?' Jeff's exasperated question broke in on his thoughts. 'I know how hard this is, Lyall, but you're not being fair.'

That did it. All his good intentions vanished, and he wheeled round to face Jeff.

'*I'm* not being fair! That's rich! Why didn't they tell me the truth? They go on and on about honesty and openness and then they pretend in front of me.'

'They thought . . .'

He was already regretting his outburst.

'I didn't even know Maddy was ill – well, apart from all those sickness bugs she gets but . . .'

'That's the cancer,' Jeff interrupted.

'Well, I know that now, don't I?' Lyall blurted out. 'But you can't kid me. I know what's going on – they don't want me living with them, because people die when I'm around!'

The daggers were sharpening themselves with glee in the pit of his stomach.

'Now listen to me!' Jeff laid an arm on his shoulder. 'That is just not true. Maybe they were wrong not to tell you sooner but they wanted to protect you. That's love, Lyall. And if you care about Maddy at all . . .'

'Of course I care!' It was out before he realised.

To his surprise, the daggers were shrinking already.

'If you do, then go home. Now. Talk to her. Tell her how much you care. Before . . .'

He hesitated.

Lyall took a deep breath.

'Before it's too late,' he finished. 'That's what you're saying, isn't it?'

Jeff nodded.

'She'll be worried sick about you, Lyall. I'll run you home – just talk to her, tell her what you told me. Tell her you care.'

'Candy, stop doing that! Candy, I'll have your guts for garters if you don't shut up! Candy, you're driving me mad!'

Mum hadn't said she loved Candy. She'd cried ever such a lot when she came to see him in the children's home; said she missed her little baby girl and all that stuff. But when she was with them, they were just 'wretched brats' or, at best, 'damn kids'.

He couldn't remember Mum ever telling Candy that she loved her.

Or him either, come to think of it.

'You're a big boy now, it's up to you to look after your sister. . . a great boy of seven wetting the bed? You'll see the back of my hand for this. . . Grief, Lyall, just shut up, can't you?'

If he hadn't been remembering, he wouldn't have let himself be nudged into the passenger seat of the car, would have opened the door before Jeff had the chance to drive off. But by the time he realised what was happening, they were in the traffic heading back up Abbey Park Avenue.

He didn't know what to say. He'd never talked to anyone about stuff like – well, love and stuff. He didn't know the words.

'She's been there for you, Lyall, for three whole years.' Jeff's voice broke in on his thoughts as the car pulled up outside his house. He leaned across Lyall and opened the passenger door.

'And now she needs you, OK?' For a moment Lyall didn't move.

'We don't need his kind of behaviour, we've got enough to cope with!'

That had been the first lot of foster parents.

'Who needs it? He should go somewhere that can deal with his outbursts!'

'I won't come in. It's down to you now,' Jeff urged.

Lyall unsnapped the buckle of his seat belt and clambered out of the car.

'OK.' He turned to slam the door. 'But what if . . . ?'

'I'll call round after the weekend,' Jeff said brightly. 'To talk about the future.'

'What future?' Lyall wanted to retort, but stopped himself. He stood watching the car disappear down the road and round the corner.

Maddy needed him.

He turned and walked slowly up the path and let himself in.

'Maddy! It's me!'

He pushed open the kitchen door. She wasn't there, or in the sitting room.

As he reached the bottom of the stairs, he heard a noise from the bathroom, a strangled cry and a lot of coughing. His heart thumping he took the stairs two at a time and threw open the bathroom door.

Maddy was leaning over the washbasin.

And there was blood everywhere.

'Maddy!' He rushed to her side, his stomach heaving. 'What . . . ?'

'Dosebleed,' she mumbled, finger and thumb tightly

pinching her nostrils. 'Won't stop!'

Her face was ashen, with tiny beads of perspiration covering her brow.

'Where's Patrick?' he asked.

'Went for a walk,' she stuttered. 'Oh, God, this won't stop!'

'OK, don't panic!' he ordered. 'Stay still – I'm going to get some ice.'

They'd done nosebleeds in the first aid training for his Duke of Edinburgh bronze award. Only not on real noses and not with real blood. No one told you blood smelt foul.

By the time he got back to the bathroom, Maddy was slumped on the floor, holding a blood-soaked towel to her face.

'Couldn't find ice cubes,' he babbled, 'so I brought this!'

He thrust a packet of frozen peas in her hand.

'You have to hold it to your nose and relax,' he told her. 'Here, I'll wrap them in a pillowcase.'

He grabbed one from the airing cupboard just as Maddy began retching and a huge blood clot shot from her mouth.

Five minutes later, the blood was still pouring. Stuff frozen peas, this was scary.

'I'm calling an ambulance!' he told her. 'Don't worry, you'll be OK – just sit still and keep spitting out the blood!'

He rushed to the bedroom and dialled 999.

'And it's urgent!' he shouted, when he'd given the details. 'I don't know what else to do. Please come!'

He felt sick but he knew he couldn't throw up now. He

turned on the tap, sat down on the bathroom floor and shyly put his arm round Maddy's shoulder while dabbing her forehead with the cloth.

'I'm so sorry, Maddy,' he said, not bothering that his eyes were wet. She wasn't about to notice things like that, what with the state she was in. 'I didn't mean to be stroppy, it's just that I – well, I care, you know, and I don't want you to die and if you have to die, I want to be around because last time...'

The front doorbell shrilled.

'They're here!' He rubbed a hand rapidly across his eyes and belted down the stairs. A burly man and a tiny girl stood on the step.

'She's in the bathroom – please help her!'

The two paramedics legged it upstairs.

'Anything we should know?' the girl asked. 'Drugs she takes, allergies, stuff like that?'

'I don't know – she's got cancer. Please help her.'

They made him stay outside on the landing. He could hear them talking gently to Maddy, hear her desperate coughing and retching and the occasional frightened sob.

'Right! Let's get you to the hospital!' the guy said, opening the bathroom door and beckoning to Lyall. 'It's not stopping so she'll need to have it cauterised.'

He helped Maddy to her feet.

'You'll clear this up, won't you, lad?' The paramedic gestured at the bloodstained bathroom.

'No!' Maddy stopped and leaned heavily on the guy's arm. 'I want my son to come with me. To the hospital.'

She lifted her pale face and looked pleadingly at Lyall.

'I'm coming,' he whispered. She'd called him her son. With no 'foster' in front of it.

He pulled himself up to his full height.

'Don't you worry, Maddy, I'm right behind you!' he affirmed. 'I'll leave a note for Patrick and then we'll be off.'

The paramedic nodded and patted him on the back.

'Got a good 'un here, haven't you, love?' he said to Maddy as he helped her down the stairs.

Lyall couldn't quite hear Maddy's reply because she was pinching her nose and smothering her face with a towel.

But he had a feeling it was something like 'the very best'.

★ ★ ★

'Fed up with waiting 4 u. C U by dodgems at 8. Scar'

Fee pressed the Delete button, rammed her phone into the back pocket of her jeans and quickened her pace towards the fairground entrance. She'd promised to meet Scarlett and Tanya and the others at seven o'clock but she'd reckoned without her parents.

She had heard the shouting before she had even opened the front door.

'You've ruined everything! I've spent my whole life covering up for you and now...'

'You've spent your whole life doing precisely what you wanted when you wanted! Why do you think I looked elsewhere? Don't come the poor injured little wife with me!'

'I had that job with the Labour Party in the bag, but now they want to put it all on hold. And why? Because of you and that little slut...'

'Don't call her that!'

'I'll call her what I damn well like!' There had been a sound very much like smashing crockery.

'I've had enough of this!' The kitchen door had opened and Fee had shot up the stairs. 'I'm going out!'

'Of course you are! Run away, why don't you? Only you needn't bother because I'm leaving you!'

Fee had been desperate to get changed and go to the Fair, but her mother's words halted her dead on the landing.

'You can't do that!' Her father's words had echoed her own thoughts.

'Why not? You don't need me...'

'What about Fee?'

Her mother's laugh had almost verged on hysteria.

'Fee?' Her voice had cracked. 'Fee doesn't like me. You know that — and it's hardly surprising, is it? I hardly spent any time with the poor kid when she was little because I was off earning money so that you could indulge in your great fantasy of being the world's greatest actor!'

'I'm very well respected...'

'Oh sure, you are now!' her mother had gone on. 'But what about all those years when you were "resting" as they call it? When I was even trying to get modelling jobs for Louise because someone had to supplement our income? And then, when Fee came along...'

The kid you didn't want, Fee had thought miserably, leaning over the banister. She had felt queasy again, but convinced herself it was because of the bickering downstairs.

'. . . when she was born, you seemed to change. Settle down. Stop flirting with every woman you ever met.'

Believe that and you'll believe anything, Fee had muttered under her breath.

'You loved it when I went off on business because you said it gave you quality time with Fee,' her mother had gone on. 'And dumb idiot that I was, I believed you! But now I discover that you . . .'

Her mother's voice cracked and to Fee's horror she could clearly hear her sobbing uncontrollably.

'That's right, rake up the past, why don't you?' Her father's trite response had fired Fee into action. She had belted down the stairs, and careered straight into her father who was storming to the front door.

'Dad! Where are you going?'

'I'll leave you to sort your mother out, Fee,' he had retorted. 'She's really hurt my feelings.'

With that the front door had slammed.

She had found her mother sitting at the pine table, her head in her hands and her shoulders shaking. A pile of newspapers had lain open at her elbow.

'Mum!' Fee had put her arm round her mother and given her a squeeze. 'Don't cry!'

'Fee, I'm sorry!'

'What for?'

'All of it!' her mother had sobbed. 'The mess I've made of everything...'

'The mess you've made!' Fee had exclaimed. 'It's Dad who keeps having affairs...'

'More than we knew about, it seems!' Her mother had pushed a copy of the *Daily Express* towards Fee. 'Look at that!'

'*I fell for love rat Richard – au pair tells all!*'

The face staring up at Fee was older but unmistakable. It was Astrid. Fee's feeling of nausea increased.

'To think that he was carrying on with her under my very nose!' her mother cried. 'How could I have been so blind? If I'd known that...'

'If you'd known, what would you have done?'

Fee had held her breath waiting for her mother's answer.

'I don't know!' she had shrugged. 'Taken you and Louise and got the hell out of here, I guess. I mean, it's one thing him flirting at parties but to do something like that under my own roof.'

She sighed deeply.

'I should never have married him in the first place – sorry, Fee, I know you adore him, but it's true. If I hadn't been...'

She had stopped in mid-sentence, pushed back her chair and walked to the window.

'If you hadn't been what?'

'Pregnant.'

Her mother's voice had been flat and expressionless.

'You were pregnant with Louise when you married Dad?' Fee had gasped, trying to get her head around the fact that her oh-so-perfect mother was human after all.

Her mother nodded.

'I didn't dare tell my parents,' she had gone on. 'You know what Granny's like – well your grandfather was ten times stricter. Luckily – or unluckily as it turns out – your father was all for marrying straight away. We lied to Mummy and Daddy – told them we had to marry in a hurry because Richard had been offered a part in a play up North.'

'Had he?'

Her mother laughed wryly.

'Oh yes – four lines and then he was murdered! But it served its purpose. When Lou was born, we got away with the old story about her being early – luckily she was quite small anyway.'

'Louise never told me,' Fee had murmured, her mind racing. If Fee was pregnant, her mum couldn't go ballistic, not now, not when she'd been in the same boat.

'Louise doesn't know,' her mother replied. 'She thinks she was a honeymoon baby. I shouldn't have told you really, but you're more level headed than your sister; she'd have made a great tragedy out of it.'

Fee sat in stunned silence. Her mother had actually said she was better than Louise at something.

Helen had picked up the newspaper and stared at Astrid's photograph.

'Listen to this: *Astrid Bertelstein, the well known German*

TV presenter and game show host, revealed yesterday that she too had been duped by Richard Bayliss when an au pair in his home. "I was young and impressionable," she said, "and when he told me he loved me, I believed him." '

Her mother had flung the newspaper to the floor.

'Stupid little fool! Thank God you never knew what was going on . . . Fee?'

Fee hadn't meant to let her expression change, but she could feel the colour flooding her cheeks as her brain re-ran the events of that night years before.

'Fee!' Her mother grasped her shoulders. 'Did you . . . are you saying?'

For some reason that was quite beyond her, Fee burst into tears.

'I'm sorry, Mum. I saw it all – but Dad said I mustn't tell a soul or I'd never see him again – and I guess I didn't really understand what was going on . . .'

'Of course you didn't, love – you were only little . . .'

'And you were away so much and Dad used to say that I was special, and I knew you loved Louise and not me and so I had to keep Dad happy, because he was all I had and . . .'

'Fee, no!' Her mother had opened her arms and pulled Fee towards her. 'That's not true, darling, honestly.'

She sat down and pulled Fee onto her lap, just as if she was eight years old again.

'But you didn't want me! I've heard you tell Dad dozens of times . . .'

'I didn't want another baby, it's true. But that was

because Dad had been flirting with other women, and spending money like water and I wanted to get out of the marriage. I could have coped with one child on my own, but two? Having another baby meant staying put; you don't mess up a child's life unless you have to.'

Fee had said nothing. The conversation had been getting too close for comfort.

'And Dad adored you on sight so I thought that you'd be – I don't know – a stabling influence on him, I guess. I told myself that for as long as I let you be his special child, he'd be faithful. Stupid me!'

'I should have told you,' Fee had whispered. 'About Astrid and the others.'

She bit her lip. Now she'd done it.

'The others – you don't mean he . . . not Ingrid and Greta and . . .'

Fee had nodded.

'I think so,' she had said. 'I mean, after that night, I never went near Dad's room, or downstairs or anything, not once I'd been sent to bed. That way, I never had to know for sure. But then he . . .'

'He what?'

Fee gulped.

'He used to come and sit on my bed sometimes and say that you weren't nice to him, so he needed lots of kind friends to help him be happy. And he wanted me to make him happy too.'

'Oh, God – he didn't . . .'

Fee shook her head vigorously.

'No, nothing like that – he just talked about how no one understood him, and how if he didn't have me to love him, he'd just walk away. So you see, I had to keep his secrets because that was the only way to keep...'

She hadn't been able to finish her sentence because she was crying so much.

Her mother had enveloped her in a breath-expelling hug.

'Oh, Fee – I'm so sorry!'

For a long while, neither of them had said a word. It had been Fee who broke the silence.

'Mum?'

'Yes?'

'You said to Dad that the Labour Party weren't giving you that job...'

Her mother had shrugged her shoulders.

'It's all about image,' she had said. 'Doesn't do to have an image consultant whose own family image has been tarnished, does it?'

She stood up.

'But I don't care,' she had added.

'You're just saying that,' Fee had smiled.

'Well, I'd have liked the kudos and the salary,' she had admitted. 'But I've been pretending for so long – maybe now that it's all out in the open, I can just be me.'

That was when Fee had sneaked a look at the clock on the mantelpiece and gasped.

'Oh, Fee, you're not off out again?' her mother had asked, making it sound as if Fee's life was one long round of jollity. 'Who with? Where are you going? Oh, not that ghastly Fair thing, surely.'

Fee had almost felt relieved to see her mother return to normal.

'Yes, Mum – the Fair,' she had grinned. 'Scarlett's meeting me.'

'Well, if Scarlett's going, I suppose that's OK,' her mother had replied. 'Such a nice girl...'

Fee didn't want to hear a catalogue of Scarlett's attributes but she did feel a bit guilty leaving her mum after everything that had happened. But if she didn't go, and Dean was there, she'd have blown her chances and right now, she knew that was the last thing she could afford to do.

Now, trying to dodge the crowds of people on the pavement, all heading towards the Fair's main entrance, she found herself scanning their faces in the hope of seeing Dean among them. She had rushed upstairs to change before her mother could say any more, and there had been no time to wash her hair or do her nails. She just hoped that her new black trousers and cream jacket gave her an air of mature sophistication.

She reached the dodgems on the dot of eight o'clock but there was no sign of Scarlett. Part of her was relieved; she knew her friend's first question would be to ask whether Fee had bought the pregnancy testing kit. She would, of course. Tomorrow. Without fail, she'd do it tomorrow.

She scanned the crowd but there was no sign of Scarlett or any of the others. She couldn't hang about; she'd told

Dean that she'd be hanging out round the scary rides. He was an adrenaline junkie; she knew he wouldn't be able to resist the roller coasters. The huge floodlights picked out pockets of people around each ride; if she began systematically looking at all the queues, she'd be sure to find him.

If he had decided to come.

'Have you seen her?' Fee jumped as a hand gripped her wrist. 'I hope you're not one of those leading her astray.'

An elderly woman with greying frizzy hair was frowning at her.

'No, you're not!' she announced. 'I haven't seen you before. I've lost her, you see.'

'Lost who?' Fee asked, not because she was remotely interested but because when someone is holding your arm in a vice-like grip, you don't have much option but to stay put.

'My daughter, dear. She's always running off, is Barbara, so full of life!'

She looked too old to have a daughter capable of running anywhere.

The woman's face clouded suddenly.

'No – not Barbara. Not looking for Barbara – there's someone else I've lost but I can't remember who it is. Do you know?'

The woman was clearly a sandwich short of a picnic.

'No,' Fee said as gently as she could. 'But you see that big white tent over there – the one with the ambulance outside? They'll help you find whoever it is.'

'No! Not the ambulance! Not that thing!'

To Fee's horror, the lady burst into loud sobs.

'I don't know what's happening!'

Fee looked around her wildly in the hope that someone would materialise and claim the woman as their own.

No one did.

'Look, I'll take you to the police checkpoint and . . .'

'Not the police! I haven't done anything and neither has Barbara. I want to go home.'

Fee had had enough.

'Come with me,' she said firmly and positively dragged the woman in the direction of the St John's Ambulance tent.

And that's when she saw him. He was pushing his way through the crowds and heading across the park to the AwesomeAwful ride.

'In here!' Fee bundled the woman through the tent flap. 'She's lost – can you look after her? She's a bit . . .'

Fee tapped the side of her forehead with her index finger.

'What's her name?' the attendant asked.

'Don't know!' Fee fled before they could rope her in to answer any more questions.

'Excuse me, mind, sorry, excuse me!' She shoved and pushed her way towards the big ride, trying to keep her eyes fixed on Dean as she did so.

'You took your time!' Scarlett grabbed her arm as she dodged past a woman with a twin buggy and a dog with a distinctly unfriendly expression on its face. 'Come on, we're all going on the AwesomeAwful – the others are saving a place in the queue. It's meant to be the best ride outside a theme park!'

'OK!' She hated fast rides, but Dean had been heading that way and if he was going on it, she was too.

'So did you see Dean?'

'Mmm,' she mumbled. 'In fact, we've just got separated – I guess he's heading this way too.'

Scarlett looked amazed.

'So it's OK between you two now?' she asked. 'Did you tell him about you know what?'

'Yes, it's OK,' Fee affirmed, praying that her wish would turn into reality, 'and no, I didn't tell him.'

She was saved from a lecture by Tanya who was hopping up and down and waving frantically in their direction.

'Come on!' she cried. 'We're on the next ride! Give me the money – I'll pay for us all.'

This, thought Fee, as they reached the towering bulk of the AwesomeAwful, is not a good idea.

'DANGER!' read the notice in three-foot high fluorescent letters. 'HIGH RISK EXPERIENCE!'

Sounds like my life, she thought wryly. The ride looked as though it lived up to its name; cars raced round at great speed, leaning and tipping, and then stopped dead and dropped almost vertically down towers, or spiralled through what they called the Corkscrew Hell.

It seemed as if half the queue was made up from Bishop Andrew kids; she spotted Verity and Ellie Clarke and a whole lot of Year Nines. Sadly there was no sign of Dean.

The shrieks and screams of those already on the ride echoed over her head and when the cars spun round and turned upside down, Fee thought she would throw up just looking at them. Scarlett was snogging with Sam, and Tanya was flirting like crazy with Wayne; they wouldn't care two hoots if she slipped off.

'Hey!' She wheeled round as someone trod on her foot in their outsize trainer. 'You can't just push in!'

'Can't we? Just did, actually!' Rick Barnes leered at her, and of course, his sidekick, Matt, wasn't far behind.

'Leave it, Fee!' Scarlett hissed in her ear. 'It's not worth messing with them.'

Fee was about to protest — she was sick of the way people gave in to the school's biggest thugs — when to her astonishment, she noticed Jay Chapman, hanging back just behind them. She couldn't imagine what he was doing; no one in their right mind chummed up with Matt or Rick, not if they valued their sanity.

'Hi, Jason!' she called, but he didn't hear her above the noise of the ride. 'Jay!'

And then she spotted him.

Dean was in the queue about fifteen people behind them, and he was with a girl. She looked about twenty-one. And his arm was round her shoulder.

She didn't want to look but her eyes seemed to be glued on his face. He was laughing and joking and then suddenly, he turned and looked straight at her.

She lifted her hand to wave, but he'd already turned away.

'Come on, it's us!' Scarlett grabbed her hand and dragged her towards the mounting platform, while Tanya shoved the cash into the attendant's hand. 'Sam and me'll go in this one – you take the one in front, then we can watch you scream!'

Fee did as she was told.

She didn't care any more.

Dean had found someone else already. Someone closer his age.

And there was nothing she could do about it.

* * *

'Get in then, Squirt!' Matt grabbed Jay's hand and practically threw him into the vacant seat beside Fee.

Ironic, really, Jay thought as he glanced apologetically in her direction. He had dreamed of being at the Fair with Fiona, and now here he was, thanks to Rick and Matt, sitting beside her and praying that she wouldn't see how scared he was.

'And you—'

Matt gestured to Scarlett and the guy she was with.

'Get out! We're taking this car!'

'You can't do that!' Jay heard the scorn in the guy's voice as he looked wildly round for an attendant, but Scarlett grabbed his hand, muttered something in his ear and dragged him further back down the ride.

'See you after, Fee!' she yelled, but Fee didn't respond. Come to think of it, she looked pretty miserable.

174

'You OK?' Jay asked.

'What? Oh, yes – fine.'

'No standing, no leaning, all safety bars locked and in place please!' The attendant shouted his orders as he checked each car.

'Scared, are you, Squirt?' Rick leaned forward and poked Jay in the shoulder as the ride moved off and began to gather speed. 'Is that why you want your nan? To hold your handy pandy on the scary rides?'

Don't respond, Jay told himself, his knuckles turning white as he gripped the safety bar.

'Ignore them!' Fee hissed in his direction. 'There's still time to get off if you . . .'

'Oh sure, like they're really going to let that happen!' Jay muttered back. 'I wasn't even here for the rides – I'm looking for my nan . . . she's gone missing and . . . oh, God!'

The ride had reached the top of the first slope and the car was hovering ready for the first, vertical plummet. Jay clenched his teeth together to stop himself from screaming as the ground appeared to roar up towards him, and the blood drummed in his ears. Then as suddenly as it had started, the dive was over.

'Why am I doing this?' Fee wailed. 'Who's gone missing?'

He hadn't meant to start on about his grandmother, but somehow it had just come out. Now there was no point in hiding anything.

'My grandmother – she gets confused, can't remember things,' he gulped, trying hard to avoid thinking about the next five twists and drops. 'I asked your mate Scarlett whether she'd seen her and those two . . .'

He jerked his head backwards in the direction of Rick and Matt.

' . . . they overheard me and started laying into me. Said I was a weed and a granny's boy and they wouldn't stop till I got on this ride.'

He gripped the safety bar and tried to ignore the fact that their car was now at the top of the first corkscrew drop.

Fee frowned.

'You shouldn't let them . . . Aaaaah! Oh no! Aaaaah!'

She grabbed Jay's hand and clung onto it for all she was worth. Terrified as he was, a warm glow flooded through him. Fiona was holding his hand!

He would have said something reassuring, but for at least a minute the power of speech left him as he fought to keep the contents of his stomach in place. And to think he'd paid £2 for this! Well, £6 actually, since Rick and Matt had demanded that he pay for them too.

He hoped they were throwing up all over one another.

'Sorry!' Fee slipped her hand out of his as the ride steadied and began climbing for the next drop. 'You were saying about your gran?'

'She wanders off,' Jay said. 'I thought she might be here because she used to bring my mum . . . oh no, this is the worst bit!'

He squeezed his eyes tightly shut and held his breath. The car leaned to an angle of forty-five, then sixty, then ninety degrees. The sky appeared to be on the ground and the trees were hanging upside down from the clouds.

'Scared are you, Midget?' Rick shouted from behind.

'No way!' He hoped they couldn't see how his hands were shaking. He turned to Fee. 'I feel sick.

She nodded as the car flipped back to its normal position and slowed slightly.

'Me too,' she agreed. 'Is your mum called Barbara?'

Jay twisted in his seat and stared at her.

'Was Barbara, yes – why? You haven't . . . ? Oh no, oh, God, helllllllp!'

They were right, he thought, as the car flung them upside down. This was the most terrifying thing he had ever experienced.

As the car righted itself once more, there was a grinding, grating sound.

'That must mean we're slowing down,' Fee sighed, and the relief in her voice was palpable. 'Listen, I think I might have seen your gran . . . oh, God, no! Help!'

For several seconds, neither of them could breathe enough to speak, because the cars were gathering speed again and lurching at all sorts of weird angles.

'I hate this!' Fee was near to tears and Jay gripped her hand again and tried to look in control.

'It's nearly over,' he said hopefully. 'You said you'd seen . . .'

Fee nodded.

'She was looking worried and talking about her daughter running off!' Fee shouted. 'Then she said it wasn't her daughter, it was someone else. I took her to the St John's Ambulance tent.'

'You did? Plump lady, frizzy hair...'

Fee nodded.

'Yes and ... oh no, here we go again.'

The cars gathered speed, rocked from side to side and then there was a loud crack.

'Hang on!' Jay yelled reassuringly. 'This is the last...'

His words were drowned by another loud crack. The car lurched and spun round and suddenly he was facing Rick and Matt.

That wasn't right. That wasn't meant to...

Another crack.

'Jason!' Fee clung onto him. 'What's happening?'

He heard Fee scream as the car lurched and tipped backwards. She was hanging head first, gripping the safety bar, her hair streaming out behind her. He stretched out and grabbed her by the arm, pulling her back with all his strength.

'Fi-o-na!'

And suddenly, he was falling forward too. He could hear people screaming, and see the watching crowds coming nearer. It would be OK; any minute now the car would swing round the right way and they'd be fine. He felt the weight of Fiona's body as it was thrown against him. For one moment, it felt like an embrace.

And then he hit the ground.

9

Lyall had been sitting in A & E for what seemed like hours. They wouldn't let him go into the cubicle with Maddy and even though they kept saying the doctor would see him in a moment, the moment never came.

He picked up a well-thumbed magazine from the corner table and flicked idly through it for the fifth time, not seeing the words on the pages. He flung it back and began pacing up and down, his eyes constantly straying to the double doors at the end of the corridor.

Where was Patrick? It had been nearly two hours since they left the house; how long a walk could he have taken?

'Excuse me!' He dodged in front of a harassed-looking nurse carrying a cardboard sick bowl and a tray of syringes. 'My mum's in there and I wondered what's going on?'

She smiled briefly.

'The doctor will be with you shortly, I'm sure,' she said.

'They said that ages ago and—'

'Look, there's a drinks machine just past the lifts – why don't you get a coffee and—'

'I don't want a flaming coffee!' he exploded. 'I want to know what's happening, OK?'

The nurse sighed.

'It's no good getting shirty with me,' she said. 'Go and ask at the desk.'

He was halfway down the corridor when all hell was let loose.

Two ambulances screeched to a halt, the glass doors were thrown open and paramedics raced past him pushing stretchers.

'Fairground accident... two teenagers... several others coming with shock and slight injuries... boy looks stable... girl bleeding heavily...'

Lyall jumped out of the way, averting his eyes from the bloodstained blanket on the front trolley.

'You wait there, sonny,' one of the paramedics was saying to the guy on the second trolley as he parked it at the side of the corridor. 'Nurse will be with you in a minute.'

'Wait! Please, you don't understand...' The guy was trying to sit up and calling after the paramedic but no one took any notice. 'It's my grand... aaah!'

He sank back onto the trolley but not before Lyall realised who it was.

'Jason? It is you, isn't it, mate?'

Jay turned, his eyes widening as he recognised Lyall.

'Lyall? Were you there too?' His face contorted in pain as he inadvertently moved his left arm.

'Was I where? What's happened?'

'The Fair,' Jay muttered. 'The roller coaster – our car broke off and... they don't understand... got to get my nan... Fee's seen her and...'

His words faded and his head lolled one side.

'Nurse! Quick!' Lyall shouted to the nearest person in uniform he could see. 'He's passed out!'

'You know him?' The nurse asked as she picked up Jay's wrist and felt his pulse. 'We need his details – he's Jason Chapman, right?'

Lyall nodded.

'Don't know much about him, though,' he said. 'He goes to my school and he wants his nan, so he says. I guess...'

'Lyall Porter!'

He turned as a tall, swarthy-complexioned doctor beckoned to him from the bank of cubicles. Lyall glanced once more at Jay's pallid face and walked over to the doctor.

'Your mum wants a word,' he smiled. 'The bleeding's stopped but don't let her move!'

'Is she going to be all right?' Lyall held his breath and held the doctor's gaze.

'Well, we'll have to wait and...'

'I know about the cancer!' Lyall's voice was steadier than his heartbeat. 'I know she's going to die. But...'

As much as he struggled to stop it, his voice broke.

'...it won't be today, will it?'

The doctor touched his arm and shook his head.

'No, it won't be yet. You've still got some time.'

'We can't hang around – there isn't time!' He remembered now – that's when the policewoman had picked him up and taken him away.

He'd cried. Said he wanted to go with Candy.

'Move it – and fast!' The paramedics had almost knocked him over in their haste to get Candy out of the flat and down the stairs.

181

'We'll go for a ride in my car – you'd like that, wouldn't you?'

He'd pinched the police lady then, kicked her as hard as he could, but she hadn't let go.

'Poor little scrap, he can't be more than six . . .'

That had made him angry because he was seven and three months.

'He'd done his best for the little lass, you could tell that . . . even managed to give her some medicine . . .'

'Hey, old chap – it's OK!' The doctor was pressing a handkerchief into his hands. 'We'll keep her in overnight and then she can go home.'

Lyall didn't tell him that it wasn't his mum he was crying over. It was those words.

'He'd done his best . . .'

Why had he never remembered that bit before? The policewoman had clearly thought he was OK. She knew he'd tried. The vicar realised it as well. People actually knew he'd tried.

The doctor tapped his arm.

'In you go and see your mum – she's been talking about you non-stop! Quite an artist, I hear!'

'She said that?'

'Sure – something about sculpture and . . . oh, here we go again! Sorry, must dash!'

He grabbed his bleeper from his shirt pocket and was halfway down the corridor before Lyall could thank him.

'Maddy?' He parted the curtains and slipped into the cubicle. She was lying with her eyes closed but at the sound of his voice, they snapped open and she grinned at him.

'Come here!' She reached out both her hands and he took them.

'Are you OK?' It seemed a dumb question under the circumstances but he couldn't think of anything else to say.

'A bit woozy, but otherwise intact!' she smiled. 'Lyall, there's something I want to tell you . . .'

'Maddy, thank God!' There was a clatter as Patrick flew into the cubicle, knocking over a chair in his hurry. 'Darling, what happened? Why the hell didn't you phone my mobile!'

'Patrick, calm down!' Maddy said. 'I had a nosebleed, but thankfully Lyall came home . . .'

'He should never have rushed off in the first place!'

' . . . he came home, and got me some ice – well, frozen peas actually . . .'

'Peas?'

' . . . and then he called an ambulance and here I am!'

Patrick slumped down onto the metal chair by her bed.

'You know what brought this on, don't you?' he snapped. 'Stress!'

His eyes rested on Lyall's face.

'You running off . . .'

Lyall held his gaze.

'It was stupid of me,' he agreed, and registered the expression of astonishment which flashed across Patrick's drawn features. 'I was all muddled up inside and I know I behaved like a dork. But then this woman said . . . Jeff made me see sense.'

'Yes, well . . .' Patrick was clearly at a loss for words.

'I love you two loads, you know!' He'd said it. He was studying the floor tiles very carefully, rubbing the toe of his trainer along the grouting.

Outside, someone called for an ECG machine. A kid in the next cubicle shrieked in fright. In the distance, a siren wailed.

'Lyall?' Maddy's voice was soft. 'Can you pop out for a minute? I just want to have a quick word with Patrick. OK?'

Sure. Nothing changed. Get rid of Lyall. He's surplus to requirements.

He pulled back the curtain.

'And Lyall love?' He turned to face Maddy. 'Don't go too far – I want you with me.'

She winked at him.

And slowly, almost as if he was carrying out a really risky dare, Lyall winked back.

★ ★ ★

'Right, young man! All in all, you were very lucky!'

The lady doctor was full of bounce as she came over to him, waving a bunch of X-rays.

'I'd hate to know what it feels like to be unlucky, then!' he replied wryly.

She grinned as the nursing sister came over to his bed.

'Well, your leg's broken, and your collar bone's fractured, but there's no internal bleeding which is good.'

'My head hurts like hell!'

'Oh, that's just a mild concussion! The painkillers will sort that,' she retorted brightly. 'Now, nurse is going to give you an injection – stop you feeling sick.'

He closed his eyes as the nurse produced a needle the size of a small pogo stick.

'This will make you feel a bit sleepy,' the nurse said. 'Just go with it.'

Jay flinched as the needle plunged into his arm.

'My friend – Fiona Bayliss – is she OK?' Another stab as the needle was pulled out.

'The tall girl with dark hair? She's in theatre now,' the doctor replied. 'I'll let you know when I have any news.'

'Theatre? She's having an operation?'

'Just checking things out,' she said vaguely. 'Your turn tomorrow!'

'Me?' Jay gasped.

'We can plaster your leg tonight, but Mr Cathcart wants a closer look at that collar bone under anaesthetic, so once we get the consent form . . .'

'I can't stay!' Jay looked at her in horror.

The registrar laughed.

'You're not in any position to go very far, are you?' she reasoned, eyeing him closely. 'Is there a problem?'

Jay sighed.

'It's my grandmother,' he began, sick and tired of having to explain the whole thing over and over again but too tired to think up any lies. 'She's – well she gets confused and she wandered off to the Fair, and my friend saw her and if I don't find her . . .'

185

'Hang on, hang on!' The registrar held up a hand. 'Ellen Rust? Plump lady, lovely smile, clearly likes shortbread biscuits . . . ?'

Jay stared at her in amazement.

'That's her! How did you . . . you mean . . . is she here?'

The registrar nodded.

'St John's Ambulance brought her in. She was clearly distressed before she saw you on the stretcher and was rather pale and breathless so . . .'

'She saw me? She'll be in an awful state. I must go . . .'

The registrar perched herself at the foot of his bed.

'Hang on! Once we get you up to the ward, I'll bring her along. But don't worry, she's as happy as happy can be!' she assured him. 'It goes like that with her condition, you know, up one minute, down the next.'

'Condition?' As he asked the question, he felt as if, suddenly, he knew the answer. Trouble was, his eyes kept closing and the room was beginning to spin and turn.

'I don't mean the breathlessness,' she replied. 'The dementia.'

'What?' Jay's stomach did a double flip.

'Surely you knew? Your parents must have . . .'

'I don't have parents!' he mumbled, trying not to slur his speech as the urge for sleep got stronger. 'It's just her and me.'

An image of the newspaper cutting swam before his eyes.

'My parents were killed . . . anyway, I thought she was just – you know, getting old, forgetful, that kind of thing.'

The registrar was staring at him.

'You mean, you haven't had any help? Age Concern? Social Services?'

He shook his head.

'No, doesn't matter though 'cos I do ve...'

He couldn't be bothered. He couldn't explain any more. The pain in his leg was floating away in one direction and he was floating in the other.

And someone else was looking after Nan.

For a while, it didn't have to be him.

He smiled to himself and fell asleep.

★ ★ ★

'Darling! You're awake!'

A large blurry blob moved into Fee's field of vision and she blinked.

'Mum?'

Her head felt about three times its normal size and her arm was throbbing violently.

'It's all right, Fee – I'm here! You're in the hospital, remember? You've been here all night.'

Flying through the air, clutching onto Jay, then pain searing through her ribs...

'The roller coaster...'

'Don't think about it! You're OK, thanks be to God – you could have been killed! They took a huge piece of metal out of your arm, and your ribs are broken but apart from that...'

'Mum, what about . . . ?'

'Your father will have to sue, of course – first thing tomorrow I'll see to it that he goes to the solicitors and . . .'

'Mum, listen. What about Jason?'

Her mother frowned.

'Jason? Who's Jason? Not that blond chap with the hideous tattoos? No, that was Dale or Darren or . . .'

'Dean? Was Dean here?'

She tried to sit up, but the pain that cut through her ribcage made her change her mind.

Her mother pulled back the curtain surrounding Fee's bed.

'Nurse! She's awake! She needs painkillers – and I think we should move her to a private . . .'

'Mum, ssshh!' Fee thought that the embarrassment was a far greater health risk than all the broken bones put together.

After the nurse had appeared, glared at Helen, taken Fee's pulse, checked the painkillers in her drip and told her that she should rest, Fee tried again.

'Dean, Mum? Was he here?'

Her mother eyed her closely.

'He was, yes,' she said slowly. 'Who exactly is Dean?'

Despite the fuzziness in her brain and the pain in her arm, she couldn't miss the caution in her mother's voice.

'Just a mate,' she said dismissively. 'Where is he now?'

'In bed, I should imagine – it is only 4 a.m., you know!'

'And you've been here all night?' Fee asked incredulously.

'Of course – where else would I be?' Her mother stroked her hair. 'When you didn't come back last night, I thought it was because of what I'd said – you know, about Dad and me not wanting babies and stuff. Then the hospital rang.'

She took Fee's hand, and dropped it again as her daughter winced in pain.

'Oh, Fee, if anything had happened to you . . . and then when I was signing the consent form, they said about the bleeding and . . .'

'Bleeding?'

'Oh, it's all right, love, it turned out it was only your period!' her mother reassured her. 'But of course, they had to check everything out, make sure nothing internal had been damaged, and all I could think about was what I'd do if . . .'

Bleeding. Her period had come. She wriggled slightly and felt the huge hospital pad between her legs. She wasn't pregnant. She waited for the feeling of elation to wash over her. Nothing happened.

'And Jason?' she asked again. 'He was in the same car on the roller coaster – he tried to catch me . . .'

'I'll find out, sweetheart. They did say something about a lad with a broken leg. Your age, is he? That's nice.'

Fee was saved from replying by the arrival of the nurse.

'Mrs Bayliss, I think you should let Fiona sleep now!' The nurse picked up the chart from the end of the bed and surveyed it closely. 'And you need to get home and rest as well – come back later in the morning!'

189

'Mum...' Fee began as her mother started gathering up her bag and coat. 'Did Dean say...?'

'He said he'd come back later, but I told him you shouldn't be disturbed!' her mother replied. 'He's clearly not your type and to be honest...'

'Mum! He's a mate!'

'Sorry, darling – anyway you get some sleep. I'll be back in just a few hours, OK?'

Fee stared at the ceiling for a long time. She wasn't going to have a baby. So now there would be nothing to keep Dean close to her.

She didn't want a baby. But she did want Dean.

But only if he wanted her. And now she was certain that he didn't.

And probably never had.

10

'I've cooked you some breakfast!' Lyall looked up as Patrick came into the kitchen. He looked exhausted, as if he hadn't slept all night.

'I'm not hungry,' Patrick sighed wearily, stifling a yawn and stretching.

'You have to eat!' Lyall ordered. 'That's what you always tell me and besides, look!'

He pulled the grill pan from the cooker and scooped sausages, bacon and rather overdone tomatoes onto a plate.

'And there's baked beans!' he added, tipping from out of a saucepan onto the plate. 'You like cooked breakfasts!'

Patrick forced a smile.

'Lyall, that's really nice, thank you! But I can't eat it all – you'll have to share it with me.'

They sat down at the table.

'You're worried about Maddy, aren't you?' Lyall remarked. 'You're angry about what she said last night.'

'No, I'm not angry!'

Lyall knew differently. He'd seen the expression on Patrick's face when Lyall had gone up to the ward to see Maddy.

'Patrick and I have been talking,' Maddy had said to him, patting the spare chair beside her and beckoning to him to sit down. 'About you – and us.'

Lyall had clenched his fists together and stared at the far wall. Here it comes, he had thought.

'When we got married,' Maddy was saying, 'we both wanted lots of kids. But it didn't happen.'

Lyall knew that – they'd told him soon after he'd arrived that they fostered people because they didn't have a family of their own.

'We've had lots of children to stay with us,' she went on, picking at the edge of the sludge-coloured hospital blanket, 'and we've always hated parting with them when the time came for them to move on.'

'Except me!' he had blurted out.

'No, Lyall,' she had stressed. 'That's the whole point. I just can't do it. I can't let you go.'

Lyall had stared at her. He'd heard it wrong, he was sure of that.

'You what?'

'If I'd had a son of my own – a birth son, I mean – well, I wouldn't have just dumped him when I got sick, would I?'

Lyall had noticed Patrick biting his knuckles and shifting uneasily in his chair.

'And I won't dump you either!' she had declared. 'We're staying together – a proper family.'

Lyall's heart had lifted.

'You mean – I'm coming to Scotland?'

Maddy shook her head.

'We won't go to Scotland,' she replied and Lyall couldn't help noticing the sigh in her voice. 'Mum and Isabel can come and see me often – you might have to move onto the sofa bed, and let them have your room but—'

'That's OK, that's fine!' He wasn't going anywhere. He was staying with Maddy and Patrick. He had felt like singing and jumping and whooping his way round the ward.

But only for a moment. Only until he caught the expression on Patrick's face, saw the pain in his eyes as he looked from Maddy to Lyall and back again.

It was that look that had stayed with him all night as he had tossed and turned in bed.

And it had only been as dawn was breaking that he realised what that look said.

'I'd be angry if I were you!' Lyall said, pushing baked beans around his plate in an attempt to cover up his loss of appetite. 'I'd be going ballistic!'

'You often do!' Patrick smiled good-humouredly. 'No, I'm not angry, it's just that . . .'

He jumped to his feet and walked over to the window, his hands stuffed into his trouser pockets.

'I just don't know if I can cope with all this!' His voice cracked. 'You can't imagine what it's like to sit by and watch someone you love dying and not be able . . .! Oh God, Lyall, I'm so sorry, I didn't think . . .'

'It's OK.' Lyall bit his lip.

'It's just that I want to wrap her in cotton wool and keep her safe and . . .'

'And have her all to yourself while you've got the chance!' Lyall finished his sentence for him.

Patrick turned round.

'Lyall, it's not that I don't want you here, and it's not that I don't love you but . . .'

'I know,' Lyall said, stabbing a sausage in an attempt to keep his emotions under control. 'See, with Candy, I didn't have a goodbye time. I didn't know she was going to die. One minute she was there, and then they took her away.'

He bit his fingernail.

'I even shouted at her that afternoon, because she threw up all over my Superman T-shirt. I wish I hadn't – I wish . . . anyway, I know what you feel like.'

Patrick nodded.

'I guess you do,' he said slowly.

'We're lucky really, you and me,' he said, fighting back the tears. 'We know we haven't got Maddy for ever, so we can make every single day special, yeah? Do the stuff she likes – go for walks, even stately homes if we have to.'

Patrick laughed.

'Now that would be self sacrifice, wouldn't it?' he grinned.

'I know I'm not easy to live with, Patrick. My temper is getting better, though, isn't it?'

He could have kicked himself for allowing the pleading tone to creep into his voice.

'You're doing great!' Patrick confirmed.

'Well, I've got the solution!' Lyall said, willing the butterflies in his stomach to stop their manic workout. 'Jeff said there's this woman who takes in kids like me and . . .'

'Maddy doesn't want you to go!'

'Hear me out!' Lyall grinned as he quoted the phrase Patrick had so often thrown at him in the middle of an argument. 'If I move in with this woman, Maddy's mum and Isabel could have my room for as long as they wanted, I wouldn't be under your feet, but I could still come round every single day and see you.'

He held Patrick's gaze.

'I could, couldn't I? I'd be really good and do all the things Maddy said and . . .'

Patrick didn't move. He didn't speak.

And then Lyall realised what a fool he'd been.

'Your new job,' he said flatly. 'You have to go, don't you? For work.'

Patrick shook his head slowly.

'The new job was just Maddy's way of protecting you, pretending she wasn't sick,' he admitted. 'I'm still looking.'

'So it could work? My plan? Couldn't it?'

For a moment, Patrick didn't move. Then he stepped forward and enfolded Lyall in a breath-expelling embrace, slapping him on the back several times.

'You know something?' he said, swallowing hard. 'You are one great guy!'

He hadn't agreed with Lyall's plan but he hadn't disagreed either.

Somehow it didn't matter.

Because, thought Lyall, he thinks I'm a great guy.

★ ★ ★

'Well now, you've got yourself in a right pickle, haven't you?'

Jay opened his eyes to see his grandmother standing at the foot of his bed. Sunlight was flooding the ward. He rubbed his eyes and tried to remember what was going on.

'You're awake!' A stout woman with tightly permed hair was standing at Nan's side, grinning broadly. 'We did come up last night, but you were sleeping.'

She turned to Jay's grandmother.

'Now then, you sit here and chat to your grandson and I'll get everything sorted out for you. Don't worry about all this contraption . . .'

She pointed to the frame that was holding the blankets off Jay's injured leg.

' . . . it looks worse than it is! How about a cup of coffee?'

'I don't drink coffee!' Nan exclaimed. 'Very bad for you, coffee. But I'd love a cup of tea!'

'Coming up!' The woman winked at Jay. 'I've no doubt she'll tell you the plan.'

If she can remember it, Jay thought, and then hated himself for his unspoken sarcasm.

'Do you hurt very badly, dear?' His grandmother looked at him solicitously. 'Did you get gravel in your knee?'

Jay smiled and shook his head.

'No gravel, Nan,' he said gently. 'I broke my leg though and smashed my collarbone, so they say I've got to stay here for a week or so. But I've told them I can't – I said I had to get home to you as soon they've seen to my shoulder and—'

'Well, it's no good you coming home!' she declared. 'Not with me off on my holidays – who would look after you? You know what you're like!'

'Holidays?' Jay stared at her. The last time Nan had gone on holiday was when he was thirteen, and they'd had a caravan in Dorset for a week.

'Oh yes!' she beamed. 'That very nice lady – I think her name's Doreen, but then it might be Dorothy... anyway, she's getting it sorted. It's a very nice place; they cook your meals and do your washing and you get outings as well!'

She tapped Jay's arm.

'It's called Recipe Care. Because I've been so busy and need to put my feet up for a while. So you're not to worry about me. You just stay here and do as you're told, you understand me?'

'Yes, Nan.' Respite care, she meant. He felt a flood of affection for her, followed rapidly by a rush of concern. What if they said she couldn't come home? What if when she did come home, she got forgetful again and...

'Well now, here we are!' The stout lady was back. 'I'm Deirdre! I won't shake your hand – might break another bone!'

She roared with laughter at her own joke.

'Now then, I expect Ellen's told you about her little holiday?'

Jay nodded.

'It is just for a few days, isn't it? Till I'm better?'

Deirdre smiled.

'She'll be back, if that's what's worrying you – but by

197

then, we'll have organised help for you – community nurses, people to pop in during the day and maybe a day centre placement. It's too much for a lad like you – you've got your own life!'

I wish, thought Jay.

Suddenly his grandmother leaned towards him.

'I'm getting a bit forgetful, Jay. I get muddled you see, and then I get scared. But after a bit of a rest, I'll be hunky-thingy again.'

'Hunky-dory!' laughed Jay. He knew she wouldn't be hunky-dory – but as long as she thought she was, that was good enough for him.

'I'll just have a word with Staff Nurse and then we'll be off then!' Deirdre said, dropping a pile of leaflets on the locker beside Jay's bed. 'These will tell you a bit about what's going on – and there's a brochure for Orchard House too – you can phone her any time and someone will bring her in to see you each day.'

Deirdre bustled off self importantly.

It's now or never, Jay thought, awkwardly shifting his bottom in bed.

'Nan, there's something I want to ask you.'

'Ask away!' she said cheerily.

'It's about Mum and the accident,' he went on warily. 'The car was stolen, wasn't it?'

For a moment, he thought his nan hadn't heard. She gazed across the room, even nodding at some of the other patients who caught her eye.

'She was a good girl, your mum!' she said, and she

sounded perfectly sane. 'That Marcus was another story!'

She sniffed loudly.

'And the car, Nan?'

'What car?'

He was about to ask another question, jog her memory about why his dad had died from a broken leg.

But he changed his mind. Why open it all up again? It wouldn't bring his parents back, and frankly, it was likely that what the papers said was the truth.

'Awful man, your father!' Nan said loudly. 'Good thing he upped and went to America, that's all I can say!'

'America? But he died!'

'No, dear, Barbara died, he just washed his hands of the whole business, upped and went . . .'

'Here we are again!' Deirdre bustled up to the bedside.

'Wait!' He held up his hand. 'Are you sure, Nan? Was it really America?'

'Was what America, dear?'

He sighed.

'It doesn't matter.' It was all probably a figment of her imagination anyway. No point worrying about it.

'Well, off we go then!' Jay was beginning to think that Deirdre might be a bit too cheery for comfort. 'I'll call in to see you tomorrow, Jason, dear, and let you know how she has settled in. OK?'

Thanks,' he smiled. 'Take care, Nan.'

He tried to hug her, which was pretty impossible with a strapped-up shoulder and a pulley on his leg.

She tousled his hair.

'See you soon, love,' she said. 'Oh, and don't stay up too late, will you?'

When they'd gone, Jay picked up a leaflet.

'Looking after a person with dementia can be exhausting... carers feel unable to relax...we give them a secure relaxed environment...meeting their individual needs.'

He felt guilty. He shouldn't be feeling happy. But he couldn't help it. His leg ached, his shoulder throbbed and his mouth was dry from all the painkillers. He was no nearer getting to the truth about his parents' accident.

But he didn't have to move. Or rush home to check out Nan. Or do the shopping, or worry about supper, or even try to fit homework in.

And just possibly, if Nan liked this Orchard House place, she could go there again and he could go to France. He wouldn't be able to have the guy back to his place, but perhaps Miss Perry would have a solution.

He could tell her the truth now.

He could tell everyone the truth.

Because the solution wasn't down to him any more.

★ ★ ★

She knew she had to ask someone. She had to find out the truth. She couldn't work out why it should matter so much, but it did.

'You're looking thoughtful!' The staff nurse picked up her wrist and began taking her pulse. 'Any pain?'

'My stomach is agony,' she said. 'Look – can I ask something? In confidence?'

The nurse pulled the curtains round the bed and smiled down at her.

'Fire away!'

'My period... I mean, it's really heavy and... when I was in theatre did they...?'

She knew she wasn't making any sense.

'I think I might have been pregnant!' She whispered the words so softly that the nurse had to make her repeat them again.

'I was late,' she hissed. 'Two weeks late and...'

The nurse picked up the chart.

'There's no mention here of a suspected miscarriage,' she said. 'Mind you, at that early stage, it would be unlikely that you'd know.'

Fee nodded.

'Thanks,' she said. 'You won't say anything, will you? To my parents or anyone?'

The nurse shook her head.

'You're sixteen, love,' she replied. 'Everything is confidential. But I will say one thing – don't get yourself into a situation where it could happen. Not at your age; it's just not worth it.'

Fee nodded again.

'I'll have to tell the doctor, though – just in case he needs to take another look, OK?'

'OK.'

She closed her eyes and lay back on the pillows. She

would never know now; she'd just have to put it out of her mind.

'Are you asleep?'

She jumped, opened her eyes and saw Dean standing at the side of her bed.

'Dean!'

She sat up, yelped in agony, and lay down again.

'Are you OK?' he asked. 'I came last night but your mother...'

'She told me!' Fee couldn't wipe the silly grin off her face. He'd come. He must love her after all. 'Don't mind her – she can be dead sniffy...'

'Anyway, I thought that before I left town, I ought to check that you were doing OK,' he went on, avoiding her adoring gaze.

'You're leaving?'

Fee's heart sank.

Dean nodded.

'I've saved up enough to get as far as Spain,' he said. 'I'll get some bar work there – Fee, it's for the best.'

Suddenly he looked a lot younger and more vulnerable than she'd ever seen him.

'If I'd known you were only sixteen, still at school, I wouldn't have got involved,' he said. 'It wasn't fair on you, I—'

'I thought you loved me!' she sobbed, all pretence at detached sophistication flying out of the window. 'I thought that when you knew—'

'Knew what?'

She bit her lip.

'That I was pregnant!' she hissed, dropping her voice so that the inquisitive woman in the next bed wouldn't hear.

Dean stared at her. He didn't speak. He just stared.

'Well, go on!' she urged. 'Say something!'

Dean shook his head slowly, his face a picture of total bewilderment.

'So all that time that we were going out, you were seeing someone else!' He stood up and turned his back on her.

'NO!' She shouted so loudly that a nurse hurried over and asked if anything was wrong.

'I'm fine!' Fee said, trying to smile. 'Just a bad twinge in the ribs!'

When the nurse had disappeared, Dean turned to face her.

'You must have been seeing someone,' he said. 'Because it clearly couldn't have been mine, could it?'

'What do you mean? Of course it could – you're the only guy I've ever done . . .'

Dean sat down in the chair and reached out a hand to touch her, before letting it drop back at his side.

'Fee, we didn't do anything! Do you honestly think I'm that dumb?'

'But the party . . .'

'Nothing happened at the party! OK, so we went upstairs, and we snogged like crazy, but I could see you were drunk and anyway, I'm not the kind of guy who goes in for unprotected sex with someone I hardly know, thank you very much!'

She was so stunned that she ignored the deprecating remark about the level of their friendship.

'Drunk? Was I really drunk?'

Dean laughed.

'And the rest! I couldn't work it out – you'd only had a couple of turbo shandies . . .'

'Turbo what? I only drank lager.'

'No, Fee, you didn't. I tried telling you that what you were drinking was lethal, but all you kept saying was, "No sweat – no probs!" I guess someone spiked your drinks – anyway, you were out of it. You fell asleep. And I swear to you on my life, nothing happened!'

Suddenly her whole body felt half a stone lighter. She felt a grin spread across her face. She was free – free of the worry, free of the fear of having to tell her parents, free of having to settle down and stick with someone . . .

The thought took her by surprise. She didn't really love him. She was fond of him, she found him sexy and funny and great to be seen around with. But love?

No.

'I hope it goes well in Spain,' she said. 'And you're right – it wouldn't have worked out.'

'Clearly not, since you had someone else! Is the baby all right?'

She shook her head.

'There was no baby! I was – well, you know, I didn't come on, and I thought that we'd . . . and we hadn't – so it was just one of those things. And now I'm fine!'

He smiled and his shoulders dropped.

'So you're OK?'

'I'm fine.'

'Great!' he said. 'I'll send you a postcard from Spain! And Fee?'

'Yes?'

'I did like you. A lot. If you really had been nineteen . . .'

She stopped him mid-sentence.

'If I really had been nineteen,' she said airily, 'I'm sure I would have found someone even sexier than you!'

He was still laughing when he waved to her from the end of the ward.

Laughing so much that he didn't see her tears.

11

'It's spectacular, Lyall!' Mrs Faber stood back and viewed the sculpture from all angles. Two hands, interlinked, reached upwards from a deep spherical hole; two hands, one large, one tiny, reached down, index fingers just touching the fingers of the upward reaching hands. Around the base of the sculpture were tiny objects – a small kangaroo, a pile of paintbrushes, a cross.

It had taken him two whole terms to get it right, but he was pleased with it. It said what he could never say with ordinary words.

'I can see that the hands reaching up and down are you and – well, those you love,' Mrs Faber went on. 'We've discussed that. But what about these objects?'

'You'll think I'm stupid,' he began.

'Lyall! We agreed you would stop running yourself down, remember?'

'OK – well, the kangaroo represents my childhood – it was my favourite toy, the paintbrushes me as a teenager...'

'And the cross?'

'I'm not saying I believe it all, because I don't!' he went on hurriedly. 'But this woman – vicar, actually – I talk to her about what's going to happen to my mum and about my sister and stuff... and it sort of helps so I put that in too.'

He paused.

'It's kind of – like, the future.'

He thought she might make fun of him, but she just nodded and walked round the sculpture yet again.

'Well, it's splendid,' Mrs Faber said. 'And after the exam, you can put it in pride of place at home!'

He nodded even though he had no intention of doing any such thing. It didn't do to let teachers in on everything, after all.

★ ★ ★

She couldn't do it. She must have been mad to think it would be OK. Just standing there in the school forecourt as the coach pulled up outside the gates was enough to bring on a fit of the shakes.

'Quick, Fee!' Scarlett nudged her. 'Get a move on – we want to bag the back seat, right?'

Wrong. The back was the worst place. Not that she was going to get on the bus. She couldn't.

She grabbed her mobile phone from the back pocket of her jeans and punched in her home number.

It rang three times before Fee realised that it was pointless. Her mother would only tell her it was something she had to do.

'Face your fears, Fiona,' she had told her the night before. 'I am.'

'Fee, come on!' Scarlett was charging up the steps into the coach, with Tanya hard on her heels.

She started to walk towards the bus.

'You go on, I'm just coming!' she called.

If she told Miss Perry she felt ill, they wouldn't risk letting her go to France. Especially if she feigned a headache, said her neck felt stiff, or that her eyes hurt when she looked at the sun.

They'd be sure to send her home.

After all, they had made Reena's parents fill in a special form before they let Reena go on the trip, and she'd been back at school for three weeks already.

France would be nice, though. It was the getting there she couldn't face.

'Hurry up, you dawdlers!' Miss Perry waved her clipboard in the direction of the last few stragglers.

Fee held a hand to her head and screwed up her eyes.

'I don't feel very well, Miss Perry,' she began. 'I think . . .'

'Excitement!' Miss Perry said. 'You'll be fine. Now get on the bus, please.'

Fee wondered whether her mother's solicitors did a good line in suing schoolteachers for lack of compassion. She would have protested but her legs were threatening to give way under her.

She had no choice but to grab the first available seat and pray.

★ ★ ★

'Can I sit next to you?' He'd said it – he knew she'd say no, say she was saving the seats for one of her mates. It was one thing to have got friendly when they were both stuck in hospital for a week, but now...

'I wish you would!' Fee looked up at Jay pleadingly. 'You're the only one who might understand.'

'Understand what?' Jay flung his holdall onto the overhead rack and dropped into the seat beside her before she could change her mind.

'I'm scared,' she confessed. 'I mean, I know it's only a coach ride, but ever since that night at the fairground...'

'Me too!' Jay admitted. 'I'm OK on buses and trains, but I can't stand going in lifts.'

'I can't bear going fast in anything – not even Mum's car,' Fee admitted. 'I feel sick and—'

'I'll look after you,' Jay said, wondering if he dared hold her hand. Probably not.

'Would you? I mean, can we hang out together? Not all the time, of course. I mean, I know you've got your mates and—'

'That would be ace!' He couldn't believe it. Fiona Bayliss and him. Together. At the same time.

'I'm scared that when we get to Poitiers, someone will suggest going to a theme park or something because if they do, I can't!'

He heard the desperation in her voice.

'Well, if they do, you and me will just do something different, right?' He grinned at her and was rewarded by hearing her chuckle.

'Yeah,' she smiled weakly. 'We'll hit the café circuit, right?'

The coach pulled away from the school amid cheers from the forty kids on board. Jay couldn't believe it. He was really going to France. Nan was in Orchard House for two weeks and Mrs Brayburn, the new carer who came in every day when she was at home, had promised to visit her and make sure she was all right. Mrs Faber had even arranged for him and Leon, the French guy, to stay with Mr Sinclair and his family when Leon came over next spring.

'If it wasn't for this wretched coach, I'd be glad to be going away though,' Fee admitted. 'My parents . . .'

She hesitated.

'I read about it,' Jay said lightly. 'It must be hard having your parents' divorce splashed across the newspapers.'

'It is,' she agreed. 'But there's one good thing – *Fiddler's Wharf* isn't shown in France, so no one will know anything about it!'

'I used to be like that about Nan,' Jay commented. 'But now I just say it like it is.'

Fee looked at him in astonishment.

'What? You just tell them that she's . . . ?'

'Got Alzheimer's. Yes, I do. It's the truth – and besides, pretending is so exhausting.'

The coach began to gather speed as it hit the M20, rocking slightly in the cross wind.

Fee snatched at Jay's hand.

'I keep remembering that night . . .' she stammered. 'Don't you wish we'd never gone to the Fair?'

Jay shook his head.

'No,' he said. 'If we hadn't gone, we wouldn't have ended up in hospital together and no one would know about my grandmother and . . .'

He stopped himself just in time.

'And what?' Fee asked

What the heck – just say it, he told himself.

'And my dream wouldn't have come true.'

'You mean, going to France?'

'No,' he said. 'I mean sitting here next to you. I think I love you, Fee.'

Like he said, pretending was just too exhausting.

Epilogue

Funny, thought Lyall, how nothing ever went according to plan. He'd imagined there would be a grave, a marble headstone with lots of fancy lettering. Instead there was just this tiny little square with a small brass plaque, partly obscured by a jug of bright yellow dahlias.

'Madeline Kent 1945–2003. RIP.'

'Here?' He looked up at Patrick, suddenly nervous that he was doing the wrong thing.

'Perfect,' Patrick nodded.

Gingerly, he lifted the sculpture from the cardboard box. Carefully he set it down beside the earth where Maddy's ashes lay. Now, a year after making it, he could see how amateurish it was; the stuff he was doing at Art College was so much better.

But this piece was the one that mattered. This was the one that had to be here.

Dropping to his knees, he moved the vase of flowers to one side and ran his finger along the bottom of the plaque.

'... and in loving memory of Candy Porter 1989–1993.'

Patrick had organised it. He'd got permission. It wasn't Candy, of course; but seeing her name there, just below Maddy's, made him feel warm.

More, he felt able to move on.

For a moment, his gaze fell on his sculpture, on the

hands reaching up to heaven and the big and small hands so confidently reaching down.

Then he stood up, turned to Patrick and grinned.

'Come on,' he said, 'let's go home.'

* * *

'It isn't there.' Jay turned to Fee, and she could hear the bewilderment in his voice.

She lifted the last of the huge books and put it back on the shelf.

'The Registry will be closing in fifteen minutes!' the tannoy boomed over their heads.

'If there's no death certificate, it means your dad is alive,' she said softly.

'So what do I do?' Jay looked at her in bewilderment.

Fee smiled.

'I guess you do nothing until you want to do something,' she said.

He looked at her gratefully.

'Of course, he might have died later; we've only looked at the five or six weeks after the accident, after all,' she added.

'Maybe.'

'Or maybe he really did go abroad and your nan just wanted to protect you from someone she thought was up to no good – who knows?'

Jay nodded.

'You know, when I realised that it was my mum who

was driving – and that she'd been drinking – I got so angry. I even—'

'What?'

'I even hated her for a bit,' he said. 'Doing such a dumb fool thing and leaving me . . .'

His voice faltered for a moment.

'The car was stolen, you know.'

Fee nodded.

'So – do you still hate her?' she asked. 'Is that why you want to find your father?'

Jay shook his head.

'I figured that I wasn't there, I don't know why she did it, or what had happened to make her drink. And I don't think I'll look for my dad.'

'Really?' Fee seemed surprised.

'He could have come to see me any time, and he chose not to,' Jay sighed. 'Nan did it all. She's the one who loved me, not him.'

'Please make your way to the exits, this office will be closing . . .' The tannoy boomed again.

'Look, I'm sorry, but I've got to dash,' Fee told him, glancing at her watch. 'I've got to catch the 5.45 train – I'm spending the weekend with Dad.'

'Doesn't your Mum mind you doing that?' Jay asked as they walked towards the exit.

Fee grinned.

'Not really,' she smiled. 'In fact, she probably won't notice I've gone.'

'What?' Jay looked startled.

'She's far too busy trying to impress the Conservative Party to notice what I do!' Fee grinned. 'Some things in life never really change!'